'Not so fast
Angelo pause

'Now that you are here, Dr Fabrielli, maybe you would have a look at another patient?'

'But of course. . .on one condition.'

Nadine stiffened. 'Condition?' She threw him a quick glance.

'Yes,' he replied smoothly. 'That you call me Angelo. After all,' he murmured, 'if we are to live together. . .'

Laura MacDonald lives in the Isle of Wight. She is married and has a grown-up family. She has enjoyed writing fiction since she was a child, but for several years she worked for members of the medical profession, both in pharmacy and in general practice. Her daughter is a nurse and has helped with the research for Laura's medical stories.

Recent titles by the same author:

DRASTIC MEASURES
FALSE PRETENCES
TOTAL RECALL

POWERS OF PERSUASION

BY
LAURA MACDONALD

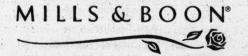

MILLS & BOON®

*First published in Great Britain 1996
Harlequin Mills & Boon Limited,
Eton House, 18-24 Paradise Road, Richmond, Surrey TW9 1SR*

© Laura MacDonald 1997

ISBN 0 263 80077 6

*Set in Times 10 on 10½ pt. by
Rowland Phototypesetting Limited
Bury St Edmunds, Suffolk*

03-9704-52065-D

*Printed and bound in Great Britain
by Mackays of Chatham PLC, Chatham*

CHAPTER ONE

NADINE HADLEY glanced in her driving mirror; the traffic seemed extra heavy that morning but she doubted that much would have changed at work during the two weeks she had been away on her course. Most of the patients would be different, of course—apart from the few long-term ones who were an inevitable part of any busy orthopaedic ward—but all the intrigues between members of staff would doubtless be the same.

Her smart blue Metro climbed the hill, leaving the centre of Hawksford far below, then swept in through the gates of the Spencer Rathbone Memorial Hospital. Nadine was glad to be back, if she was honest. She loved her job as Senior Sister on Orthopaedics and, even though she had found the course in new nursing techniques and communication skills something of a challenge, she was happiest in her own environment.

Humming along with the car radio, she drew into the staff car park and headed for the bay which was unofficially reserved for her. Driving forward at an angle—a well-rehearsed manoeuvre executed countless thousands of times—Nadine was about to reverse when she saw that a motorbike was parked in the space. It was pretty obvious that it had only just arrived for its rider was still seated and had not even switched off the engine.

Muttering under her breath, Nadine wound down her window. 'You can't park there,' she said, shaking her head.

The rider, clad entirely in black leather, was still wearing his crash helmet. He tilted his head questioningly to one side and Nadine realised that he couldn't hear her because of the noise of the engine. She shook her head

5

again, irritated now and hoping that he would get the message and move, but to her further annoyance he switched off the engine, dismounted and walked towards her.

'I'm sorry?' he said, lifting the visor of his crash helmet.

Nadine found herself looking into a pair of eyes so dark that they appeared almost black. 'You can't park there,' she said, nodding towards his motorbike.

'I can't?'

There was an accent in his voice that for the moment Nadine couldn't place. 'No, this is the staff car park— the public one is over there.' She pointed to the far side of the hospital grounds.

He appeared to hesitate for a moment then he stared intently at her, at her car and then back towards the space. 'Ah,' he said. 'This is your space.'

Nadine nodded.

'Sorry.' He raised his hands in a submissive gesture and, as he walked back to his bike and remounted, Nadine could not help but notice what a magnificent machine it was. It, too, was black, with gleaming chrome-work, and as he moved forward she saw the name Harley Davidson emblazoned on the side. Briefly the thought crossed her mind how much her son, Paul, would love such a machine, then the thought was gone—along with the rider, who raised his hand before disappearing in a low, powerful roar in the direction of the public car park.

Ten minutes later Nadine had all but forgotten the incident as she changed into her uniform and prepared once more to take up the reins of the busy orthopaedic unit. She was joined in her office by her two senior staff nurses, Jayne Reynolds and Ruth Stannard, as the rest of the staff began to gather outside at the nurses' station to take report from the night shift.

'How did the course go?' asked Jayne, securing her fob watch.

'Not too bad,' said Nadine, 'but it was tiring.'

'These courses generally are.' Ruth glanced into the mirror on the office wall, checking her hair as she spoke.

Nadine stared at her. Ruth was usually rather staid and a bit old-fashioned but today there was something different about her, although, for the moment, Nadine couldn't think what it was. 'Yes, well, I'm glad to be back,' she said. 'So, tell me, what's been happening around here? Anything much?'

The two nurses glanced at each other, then Ruth looked at the floor and it was Jayne who answered. 'Not a lot, really,' she said. 'Barry Fletcher is still here, following his spinal surgery, and young Josh Barnes is still in traction after his accident. I think those are the only two who were here when you went away. Everything else is pretty straightforward, I think—the usual crop of hip replacements, knee joints and fractures.'

'And the staff?'

'Staff?' Jayne looked up.

'Yes,' said Nadine. 'You've taken care of the patients; what about the staff? What's been happening with them while I've been away?'

'You think something might have been happening?' Jayne grinned.

'In my experience,' said Nadine wryly, 'the patients are always the least problem. It's the staff who pose the most complicated situations.'

'Really?' Jayne's eyes widened innocently, but merriment lurked near the surface.

'Yes,' said Nadine firmly. 'So let's start with you. How's John?'

'Fine.'

'And that gorgeous baby of yours?'

Jayne laughed. 'Yes, Reece is fine too.'

'Good. So that's you OK. Ruth?' She glanced at her other staff nurse.

'Oh, I'm all right,' Ruth sniffed. 'Same as always.'

'Good.' Nadine shot her another swift glance. There

was something different. She was sure of it, but she still couldn't quite put her finger on what it was. 'And the others?' she said crisply.

'Well,' said Jayne slowly, pulling a face, 'now we come to the crunch...'

'Oh, no,' said Nadine with a groan, 'I thought there was something... Come on, let's have it... Who is it?'

'There are two of them, actually,' said Jayne.

'Two of them...?'

'Yes, Lee and Karen...'

Nadine frowned. 'So, what's wrong with them?'

'They're in love.'

'Both of them?'

Jayne nodded. 'Afraid so.'

'Oh, God, no,' said Nadine. 'Anything but that. And you say both of them?' She stared in mock horror at Jayne, vaguely aware that Ruth, with a muttered excuse, had left the office. When Jayne nodded, she went on, 'We have enough problems when it's one...but two, and on the same unit and at the same time! I wish I'd stayed on my course.'

'You haven't heard the half,' said Jayne with a dry chuckle.

'You mean there's more?' Nadine stared at Jayne and saw that she was struggling to keep a straight face.

'Much more,' she replied solemnly.

Nadine sighed and sat down behind her desk. 'Well, go on,' she said when Jayne remained silent, 'let's have it. Let's hear the worst.'

'Well,' Jayne began patiently at last, 'not only are Lee and Karen both in love. Believe it or not, they are both in love with the same man.'

'Oh, for goodness' sake!' Nadine stared at her in growing exasperation, then she frowned. 'You're not joking, are you?' she said at last in a resigned sort of voice.

Jayne shook her head.

'I suppose in a minute you're going to tell me that

this man, whoever he is, is a member of staff. . .'

'Funny you should say that, Nadine. . .' said Jayne, raising one eyebrow.

'Oh, come on. Be serious.' Nadine stared at Jayne. 'I was joking!'

'Well, I'm not.'

'So, who is he, for heaven's sake? I can't think of anyone who could possibly fit that particular bill at the present time.'

'That's because you haven't met him yet.' Jayne grinned.

'So, who is he?' Nadine was aware that outside the rest of the staff were congregated, and were waiting for Jayne and her to join them. 'Come on, tell me.'

'The new registrar.'

'Ortho?' Nadine's eyes widened.

'Yep.'

'Oh, great!' She turned away, exasperated. 'So, not only is he a member of staff but he also just happens to be here on the very unit as the two nurses who are throwing a wobble over him. My unit!'

Jayne nodded ruefully and pulled a face.

'Who is he?' Suddenly Nadine was curious, in spite of herself. 'This God's gift to women?'

'He's Italian,' said Jayne then, seeing Nadine's look of surprise, explained, 'Apparently he's here on a temporary contract—a protégé of Seymour Russell.'

'I suppose that's the attraction,' said Nadine, 'the fact that he's Italian.'

'I have to admit he is very dishy,' said Jayne with a laugh. 'And he's nice with it. . .'

'I can't help that,' said Nadine crisply. 'I don't want anyone causing chaos amongst my nurses, whoever he is. . . Speaking of which,' she narrowed her eyes and looked through the glass partition that separated her office from the ward beyond, 'there's something different about Ruth. . . What is it?'

Jayne laughed. 'So you've noticed. She's had high-lights put in her hair.'

'Ruth? Highlights?' said Nadine in disbelief.

Jayne nodded.

'When did she have that done, for heaven's sake?'

'About a week ago. Just after Angelo Fabrielli arrived, in fact. . .'

'Angelo Fabrielli. . .?' Nadine frowned, then looked sharply at Jayne. 'You mean. . .?'

'You've got it,' said Jayne. 'That's the one. You'll meet him on ward round.'

'I can't wait!' groaned Nadine.

During report Nadine brought herself up to date with the patients on her ward—those awaiting surgery that morning and those recovering—then, after report, she did a tour for herself, inquiring and reassuring.

One patient, eighteen-year-old Josh Barnes had been on the ward for three weeks, following a motorbike accident. When Nadine had left to go on her course he had been in a very critical condition with multiple injur-ies, including fractures to both legs and one arm and head and internal injuries. Today, when she reached his bed, she looked at him with a smile, then picked up his chart.

'This is certainly an improvement on the last time I saw you,' she said. 'In fact, I doubt you even remember seeing me at all.'

'I do, as it happens,' said Josh with a grin.

'You do?' Nadine was surprised. 'You were in a pretty sorry state when they sent you up here from Casualty.'

'I know,' said Josh, 'but I remember when I came round after my op—you were there. I thought you were my mum.'

'Quite a disappointment when you found I wasn't?' Nadine laughed.

'Not really. You didn't moan at me for driving too fast.'

'And your mum did?'

'Yes.' Josh pulled a face.

'All mums have to do that,' said Nadine. 'I'm here to make sure you get well. Your mum has to make sure you don't do it again.'

'You sound like you know.'

'I have a son who is motorbike-mad,' said Nadine with a grimace.

'How old is he?' asked Josh with interest.

'Sixteen.'

'Has he got a bike yet?'

'No,' Nadine shook her head, 'but I have an awful feeling that the day will come. Now, Josh—' she glanced back at his chart again '—the doctor will be round to see you soon. I understand you had some pain during the night?'

Josh nodded and the muscles around his mouth tightened.

'Well, we'll see what the doctor recommends,' said Nadine.

'Those painkillers are useless,' said Josh in disgust. 'They've worn off after about a couple of hours.'

'Maybe the doctor will suggest changing the dose or trying something a bit stronger,' said Nadine.

'Right.' Josh nodded then, lowering his voice, he said, 'Have a word with the old boy in the next bed will you, Sister? He's come in to have his knee done. I think he's scared, although he won't admit it. I told him there's nothing to be afraid of—after all, look what I've had done—but I don't think he was convinced.' He raised his head from the pillow and looked sideways. 'Here he comes now,' he said. 'He's a funny old chap. . . He's just been to the loo. . .again; that's about the tenth time!'

'All right, Josh,' said Nadine, 'I'll have a word.' She moved on to the next bed where the patient, an elderly man, was bending over his locker.

'Good morning,' Nadine said brightly. 'Mr Norman, isn't it?'

The man looked over his shoulder, peering at Nadine through a pair of thick-lensed spectacles. 'Have I got to go now?' He looked alarmed.

'Go where, Mr Norman?' asked Nadine.

'For my operation,' he said. 'I'm having an operation this morning, you know, on my knee.'

'Yes, I know you are.'

'How do you know?' he frowned. 'I haven't seen you before, have I?'

'No, Mr Norman, you haven't,' replied Nadine patiently, 'because I've only just come on duty, and I wasn't here yesterday when you came in. I'm Sister Hadley.'

'Oh, I see.' He blinked. 'So, are you in charge around here?'

'Yes.' Nadine nodded, then briskly she went on, 'Now, are you quite happy about everything?'

'Well, I wouldn't say that exactly,' said Mr Norman.

'Oh, I'm sorry to hear that.' Nadine cast a critical eye over his bed, noting that it had already been made up ready to receive him back from Theatre. 'What's the problem?'

'Well, would you be happy if you were going to have your knee hacked about?' Mr Norman barked, glaring at her, his eyes huge through the highly magnified lenses of his glasses.

'Probably not,' admitted Nadine, 'but I would try and concentrate on how much better I was going to be afterwards.'

'That remains to be seen.' He continued to stare at her then he turned back to his locker, mumbling away to himself as he did so.

'There's nothing to worry about, Mr Norman,' said Nadine gently. 'Really, there isn't. You've got an excellent surgeon and you're having a general anaesthetic, so you won't know anything about it.'

'Not one of these young fellow-me-lads doing it, is it? Still wet behind the ears, some of them.'

'Mr Russell is doing your operation, Mr Norman,' said Nadine. 'He's one of the leading orthopaedic surgeons in this country,' she explained. 'He's done hundreds of knee replacements and always has excellent results. Now, have you had a bath? Good. And got your gown on?' She lifted back the collar of his green plaid dressing-gown. 'Good. In that case, what I would like you to do now is pop up on your bed, and Nurse will come along in a minute to give you a pre-med.'

'What's that?' Immediately Mr Norman looked suspicious.

'It's an injection—'

'Injection?' His head jerked up in alarm.

'To help you to relax,' said Nadine firmly. 'Now, tell me,' she said as she drew the curtains and helped him on to his bed, 'has the anaesthetist been to see you?'

'Young whippersnapper with a bow tie?' asked Mr Norman.

'Mr Farrington, yes.' Nadine struggled to keep her face straight. 'Good. Well, I want you to rest now, Mr Norman, so I'll leave the curtains drawn around your bed.'

'My wife will think I've died if she comes in,' he said.

'Your wife won't be in yet,' said Nadine. 'And by the time she does you'll be sitting up in bed eating your supper.'

As she stepped from behind the curtains she caught Josh's eye, saw the gleam of amusement there, frowned warningly and then turned as Jayne called her.

'Doctors' round, Nadine,' Jayne said. 'They'll be here in ten minutes.'

'Thank you, Jayne.' Swiftly Nadine moved down the ward, nodding to the patients she hadn't yet had a chance to speak to and casting a critical eye over everything as she went to ensure that the high standards she set had been maintained during her absence.

In her office she checked that the appropriate patient records were ready in the trolley, and as she passed the mirror she paused to check that her frilly white cap was straight. A strand of her ash-blonde hair had worked loose from the tortoiseshell slide she used to secure it at the nape of her neck and she tucked it firmly back into place, lingering a moment to scrutinise her appearance.

Steady grey eyes stared back at her above a short straight nose and a determined chin. She wore a minimum of make-up for work, just enough to bring a touch of colour to her delicate complexion. This morning, however, she seemed extra pale. Maybe, she thought, a touch of blusher to her cheeks would help.

She was just lightly applying the brush to her cheekbones when Jayne opened the office door, tapping on the glass as she did so. She grinned when she saw what Nadine was doing.

'Got to you as well, has he?' she said.

'Who?' Nadine frowned and slipped her brush back into her make-up bag.

'The new reg.'

'Hardly.' She pulled a face and put the make-up bag inside her handbag, which she tucked away out of sight under her desk. 'Besides, I haven't even set eyes on him yet and, when I do, I doubt he'll make any impression.'

'You wait.' Jayne laughed. 'I tell you, if I didn't have my John. . .'

'So how old is he, this Romeo?' Nadine raised one eyebrow.

'Twenty-six, twenty-seven. . .I'm not sure really.'

'A mere infant,' sniffed Nadine. 'Besides, I've always preferred older men.'

'Like Seymour Russell, you mean?' Jayne grinned. It was a well-known fact on Orthopaedics that on occasion Nadine went out with the senior consultant surgeon.

'There's nothing like that between Seymour and me,' replied Nadine crisply, 'as you very well know.'

'Well, I think it's a shame,' said Jayne. 'I reckon it's high time you had a man in your life again.'

'I don't think so.' Nadine shook her head. 'I settle for a peaceful existence these days—at least, as peaceful as is possible with a sixteen-year-old in the house.'

'I still think it's a shame. . .' Jayne stared thoughtfully at her, her head tilted to one side.

'You sound like my mother,' laughed Nadine. 'She's always trying to pair me up with someone. She has parties and invites all her arty friends. I know beforehand that there will always be a spare man, hovering around. . .' She trailed off at the sound of approaching footsteps.

'Here we go,' breathed Jayne as Seymour Russell suddenly appeared in the office doorway, his little band of registrars, housemen and medical students hovering deferentially behind him.

'Good morning, Sister, Staff Nurse.' Seymour peered over the top of his bifocals at Nadine, then at Jayne.

'Good morning, Mr Russell,' Nadine smiled. She was fond of Seymour but she really hadn't been exaggerating when she'd told Jayne that that was all there was to their relationship.

'Nice to see you back,' Seymour went on. 'How was the course?'

'Like most other courses, I suspect,' replied Nadine. 'At the time you think you'll never take everything in— it's only afterwards that you find yourself wondering if you've actually learnt anything you didn't already know.'

'Ah, but it would have been presented in an entirely different way,' said Seymour, moving aside for Nadine and for Jayne—who was pushing the record trolley— to join the group.

'I can see you've been on these courses as well,' said Nadine.

Seymour laughed, amidst a polite ripple of amusement from the others. Nadine moved forward and glanced round. 'Good morning, ladies, gentlemen,' she said, and would have moved on to the first patient but Seymour spoke again.

'I'm sorry, Sister,' he said, 'I was forgetting. You haven't met my new registrar, have you?'

'No, I haven't,' said Nadine, suddenly curious, in spite of herself, after all she had heard about the man. She turned just as a man stepped forward from the back of the group.

'This is Dr Fabrielli, Sister,' said Seymour. 'He is with us from Rome for a short time... Dr Fabrielli, Sister Hadley.'

Her first impression was of a man taller than herself— a young man of slightly stocky build with very dark hair that curled against the collar of his white coat and a smooth, tanned complexion with just a hint of shadow around the jaw. But, as he took her outstretched hand, what struck Nadine the most was the sudden awareness of having met him somewhere before. She had no time, however, to even consider where or when this might have been because Dr Fabrielli spoke first.

Bending over her hand, he said, 'Sister Hadley and I have already met, even though it was only very briefly.' He spoke English perfectly but with a strong Italian accent.

Nadine frowned. That accent...she'd heard it somewhere, somewhere recently—very recently—but had not at the time recognised it as Italian. She only had a split second to wonder, not really long enough, for he looked up then and as she stared at him his eyes provided the answer. Eyes so dark that they appeared almost black. Eyes she'd seen only a short while ago but which, on that occasion, had been gazing under the visor of a crash helmet.

'You're the man with the motorbike.'

'The very same,' he murmured.

'You've already met?' Seymour sounded amazed.

Nadine nodded. 'Yes, but, as Dr Fabrielli said, it was very briefly.'

There was an awkward little silence as if no one knew quite what to say, then Seymour noisily cleared his throat. 'Shall we get on?' he said.

'Yes, of course.' Without another glance at the registrar, Nadine moved to the foot of the first patient's bed but, as she gave the report and watched while Seymour examined the patient, her mind was racing.

Why hadn't the man told her that he was a doctor, for heaven's sake? Because she'd never seen him before, she had automatically assumed that he was a member of the public. How could she have known that he was a member of staff and one so new that he had joined the staff in the short time she had been away?

'How far are we now, Sister, since Mr Fletcher's fusion?'

Nadine glanced up sharply as she realised that Seymour had spoken to her and she'd hardly heard him. She was in time to see a half-smile on Dr Fabrielli's lips. Annoyed, she turned her attention to Seymour and the patient, Barry Fletcher.

'This is the start of the third week,' she replied crisply.

'Any problems?' Seymour looked over his glasses.

'Any problems, Staff Nurse?' Nadine glanced at Jayne, who had been Acting Sister while she'd been away.

'Not really,' replied Jayne. 'Not once pain had been adequately controlled and constipation had been sorted out.'

'Good,' said Seymour, 'although I suspect Mr Fletcher may give a different answer.'

Barry Fletcher grinned. 'I think I'm almost beginning to get used to lying flat,' he said. 'I've been conducting a survey into the number of cracks in the ceiling.'

'Not much longer to go,' said Seymour with a hearty laugh.

Nadine passed the records to Seymour, and as he

made some notes she found her thoughts wandering
back to the incident in the car park. The new registrar
had made her feel foolish. He should have told her who
he was. They had had a lot of trouble with members of
the public parking in the staff car park, and her mistake
had been quite understandable. But he should have said.

Nadine had the distinct impression that he had known
exactly who she was. He might have known that it would
cause embarrassment when she found out who he was.
On the other hand, there was just the chance that he
hadn't known, in which case she supposed that she really
should be prepared to give him the benefit of the doubt.

They moved on down the ward. At her request,
Seymour had a reassuring word with Cyril Norman—
relaxed now after his pre-med—then adjusted Josh's
medication. When the ward round was almost over,
Nadine happened to intercept a glance between Lee
Bevan, one of her junior staff nurses, and the new
registrar.

At any other time she might not have noticed but this
morning, because of what she'd been told and because
of her own embarrassment with the man, she found
herself more irritated than the incident really warranted.

Lee—red-faced—realising that Nadine had seen,
retreated to the sanctuary of the sluice, while Seymour
announced that it was time he and his theatre team got
scrubbed up.

Nadine escorted the doctors to the ward entrance but,
as she turned to go back to her office, it suddenly
occurred to her that the new registrar hadn't been among
the group.

Nadine stiffened. Surely he hadn't followed Lee into
the sluice? Maybe he had become used to that sort of
laxness during her absence, she thought. Well, if he had,
he could think again. Angrily she set off down the ward
towards the sluice, but as she passed the open door of
her office she caught a glimpse of a white coat.

She stopped and, going back, looked round the door.

Dr Fabrielli was lounging against her desk, flicking over the pages of a medical journal.

He glanced up as she came right into the room

'Ah, Sister,' he said with a smile, no doubt intended to devastate. 'A word, if you please.'

'Shouldn't you be getting scrubbed up, ready for Theatre?' she enquired briskly. 'The list starts shortly, and Mr Russell can't abide lateness.'

'I am not assisting Mr Russell today,' he replied smoothly.

'Oh, I see,' said Nadine. 'Well, I hope this won't take long, Dr Fabrielli. As I'm sure you can appreciate, I am very busy this morning—having been away for two weeks.'

'I know,' he said softly, his dark eyes meeting hers. 'And that was what I wanted to see you about. Your being away.'

'My being away?' Nadine frowned. 'I don't understand.' She couldn't imagine what her being away could have to do with him.

'Yes,' he said, 'because, while you were away, I used your space in the staff car park. That is why I was there this morning. It is my fault; I am sorry. I should have realised who you were as soon as I saw you, and I should have moved.'

'You should have told me who you were,' said Nadine quickly, 'when I mistook you for a member of the public and sent you off to the other car park.'

'Even if I had, I would have to have gone.' He smiled, again that disarming smile. 'There were no other spaces in the staff car park.'

'Even so. . .' She gave a slight shrug.

'I did not want us to get off to a bad start,' he said.

'No, well. . .' Nadine trailed off, embarrassed now more by the look in his eyes than by the misunderstanding. 'Anyway, I must get on,' she muttered. 'If you'll excuse me, Dr Fabrielli.'

'Of course, Sister.' Again the charming smile and

then, to Nadine's relief, he turned and left the office.

Taking a deep breath, she turned to her desk and the mountain of paperwork which awaited her. Dr Angelo Fabrielli might think he only had to flash one look at her nurses from those smouldering eyes of his to have them swooning all over him, she thought grimly, but if he thought that sort of behaviour would cut any ice with her he could think again.

CHAPTER TWO

WHEN the shift was over Nadine left the hospital with Jayne, and together they walked to the car park. There was a decided nip in the air, in spite of the bright mass of April flowers in the hospital gardens, and Nadine pulled her wool jacket more closely around her.

'Are you going out tonight?' asked Jayne.

'I'm not sure,' replied Nadine. 'I've got a few things to catch up on at home after being away.'

'No dates with Seymour, then?' Jayne smiled.

'At the weekend, yes, as it happens. He's asked me to go to the theatre with him.'

'Really?'

'You can take that grin off your face,' said Nadine, 'because I can assure you that's all it is—a theatre date.'

'Talking of dates,' said Jayne, 'Lee has just told me that she went out with Angelo Fabrielli at the weekend—that'll put Karen Ashton's back up.'

'Well, I hope she knows what she's doing,' said Nadine crisply. 'Our Italian friend is too much of a charmer for my liking.'

'True,' agreed Jayne as they reached their cars, which were parked alongside each other, 'but he is gorgeous. You have to admit that, Nadine—all that smouldering Latin passion.'

'I suppose so.' Nadine laughed.

'What was all that about his motorbike?' asked Jayne. 'Did you catch him parking in your space?'

'Yes,' Nadine nodded, then quickly added, 'but I didn't know who he was at the time. I thought he was a patient or a visitor or something. I was a bit sharp with him, actually—I sent him off to the public car park. I felt a bit silly when I found out who he was.'

21

'He asked me if he could park his bike in your space,' said Jayne, 'only, of course, he didn't know then that it was your space. I told him, then said it would probably be all right, but only until you returned—then you would be wanting it back.'

'Oh, well, he must have found somewhere to park.' Nadine fitted her key in the lock, then looked across the car roof at Jayne. 'That's a pretty pretentious bike he has there.'

'Yes,' Jayne nodded, 'it is. He said he uses a bike because it's easier in traffic. . .'

'Yes, but a Harley Davidson. . .'

'I know.' Jayne laughed. 'Someone said he comes from a very wealthy family.'

'He must do. Registrars don't earn that much. I hope Paul doesn't see that bike—I'd never hear the last of it.'

'How is Paul?'

'Still motorbike-mad.' Nadine pulled a face. 'I just wish he'd go off the idea. I keep threatening to bring him in here—into Casualty preferably—and let him see the accident victims—kids like Josh Barnes.'

'Might just have the opposite effect,' said Jayne, opening her car door.

'I know.' Nadine sighed. 'Perverse creatures, teenagers. And at the moment GCSEs have to take priority. Anyway, I'd best get on; see you tomorrow, Jayne.'

Moments later she drew out of the staff car park, reaching the junction with the public car park at the precise moment that Dr Fabrielli drove out on his Harley Davidson. He stopped when he saw her and, with an exaggerated gesture, allowed her to proceed first. Nadine nodded coolly in response and drew away but some time later, while negotiating Hawksford's rush-hour traffic, she glanced in her driving mirror and found the black motorbike, with its leather-clad rider, still behind her.

'Who does he think he is?' she muttered to herself, 'He comes over here from Italy, flashes his money around and buys the most expensive bike going—and, if that wasn't enough, he chats up all my nurses and looks fair set to break their hearts into the bargain.' She was still muttering when she next looked in her mirror to signal that she was turning left into Acacia Avenue. As she carried out the manoeuvre and Dr Fabrielli roared away, to her further irritation he raised one hand in farewell.

Home for Nadine and her son, Paul, was the top floor of Montague House, a large, detached, red-brick Victorian villa. The ground and part of the first floor was occupied by Nadine's mother, Fiona. Her father, Desmond, had died of a stroke two years previously, shortly after retiring from his job as a radiographer. Nadine still missed him desperately.

She parked her Metro on one side of the wide shingle drive behind her mother's small green Fiesta, and switched off the engine. Getting out of the car, she ducked to avoid the branches of the flowering cherry trees beside the drive which had already begun to shed their petals in recent high winds.

When she entered the house Nadine could hear Paul in the kitchen, talking to her mother, so, instead of going straight upstairs to her flat, she walked down the hall and pushed open the kitchen door. Paul was sitting at the large central table, surrounded by his school books. A tin of his grandmother's home-baked biscuits stood open in front of him, together with a large mug of tea. He looked up as Nadine entered the room.

'Hi, Mum!' He smiled. It was Julian's smile, and the similarity between father and son gave Nadine a sudden pang. The likeness hadn't been so apparent when Paul had been a little boy but now that he was nearly a man, and approaching the age Julian had been when she had known him, it was unmistakable. The same dark hair that flopped over his face, the fine-textured skin and the same serious, dark eyes.

'Hello, love,' she said. 'Had a good day?'

'Not bad.' He wrinkled his nose. 'I got a B for that Evolution project.'

'And were you happy with that?' asked Nadine, knowing full well what his reply would be.

'No, I wanted an A.'

'Is that you, dear?' Her mother's voice called from outside.

'Yes, it's me,' Nadine called back, watching Paul as he bent his head over his work again and only looking up as her mother appeared in the open doorway. The back of the house caught the afternoon sunshine, and many years ago her father had built a conservatory to house his beloved geraniums and begonias.

Since his death Nadine's mother, Fiona—or Fee, as everyone called her—had done her best to keep the blooms going, knowing that would be what Desmond would have wanted. She stood now in the doorway—a petite woman of sixty with fading blonde hair, a dreamy smile and the same silver-grey eyes as her daughter.

'Had a good day, dear?' Anxiously she asked the same question that Nadine had of Paul.

'A bit fraught.' Nadine pulled a face. 'First day back and all that.'

'I bet something had changed,' said Paul suddenly.

'How do you mean, ''changed''?' Nadine looked down at him again.

'While you were away. I've noticed that, you know,' said Paul seriously. 'If you're away, even if it's only that you've been sick for a couple of days, when you get back something will have changed—it's really weird, that.'

'Yes, it is.' Nadine nodded. 'But I know exactly what you mean.'

'So, what was different?' asked Fee, crossing to the Aga and moving the kettle onto the hob to boil.

'Well, most of the patients had changed, of course, but the biggest difference was caused by the fact that we have a new registrar.'

'Hadn't you known about that?' asked Fee, spooning tea into a brown china teapot. 'Before you went on your course, I mean.'

'Yes, I had heard mention of it,' Nadine nodded, 'but I'd forgotten.'

'Is Josh Barnes still there?' asked Paul. Josh, two years older than Paul and in the sixth form at his school, had become something of a folk hero since his accident.

Nadine nodded. 'Yes, he's still there,' she said, then added grimly, 'and likely to be for some considerable time.'

'So, what's he like?' Fee poured boiling water onto the tea, peered into the pot then put the lid on.

'Who, Josh Barnes?' Nadine, watching her, smiled faintly.

'No,' Fee replied seriously, 'your new registrar.'

Paul smiled at Nadine and bent his head over his books again.

'Well, he's a bit different from the usual type we get, I must admit,' Nadine said slowly.

'In what way?' Fee liked to hear any gossip from the hospital—the sort of gossip that Nadine was able to tell her without breaching confidentiality.

'For a start, he's Italian,' said Nadine. 'I don't think we've had an Italian doctor at Spencer Rathbone before—just about every other nationality, but not Italian.'

'Is he handsome?' asked Fee. 'They usually are, Italian.'

'Oh, he's handsome all right,' said Nadine wryly, 'and he's got most of my nurses fighting over him. I foresee all sorts of trouble on Ortho before too long.'

'How romantic,' sighed Fee, pouring tea into a mug and handing it to Nadine.

'Not for me, it isn't!' Nadine retorted. 'I shall be the one who has to sort it all out, you mark my words. And as if his looks weren't enough,' she sniffed when Fee

declined to comment, 'rumour has it he's wealthy
as well.'

'Wealthy?' Fee raised her eyebrows at that. 'Are
registrars usually wealthy?'

'No. So it's just one more thing that will make him
interesting.'

'Maybe you're mistaken.' Fee frowned. 'What makes
you think he's wealthy?'

'He must be reasonably well off to ride a Harley
Davidson,' said Nadine. The minute she'd said it she
wished she hadn't, because Paul's head shot up again.

'Did you say Harley Davidson?' He gaped at her,
open-mouthed.

She nodded in an offhanded sort of way, she hoped,
and sipped her tea. 'A great black monster of a machine,'
she said.

'Wow!' breathed Paul.

Nadine caught her mother's eye and by mutual,
unspoken agreement the subject was changed.

'Do you want me to cook supper tonight?' asked Fee.

'Have you got a rehearsal?' asked Nadine and when
Fee nodded, she said, 'In that case, I'll get ours. You
just get yourself ready.' Fee was deeply involved in
local amateur operatics, and rehearsals were well under
way for the company's latest production. 'I think I'll go
up to the sports centre later for a swim.' Nadine glanced
at her watch.

'I'll come with you,' said Paul quickly.

'OK.' Nadine nodded and drained her mug. Secretly
she was pleased that Paul should still sometimes want
her company.

Leaving her mother and Paul, Nadine made her way
upstairs to her flat. Large, airy rooms led into each
other, bright with the last of the afternoon's sunshine
and indelibly stamped with her and Paul's personalities.
Cool white walls contrasted strongly with the bold Aztec
print of the curtains and the masses of cushions scattered
on the deep, squashy sofa and on the floor,

Bright posters and a few good French impressionist prints adorned the walls of the sitting-room, the kitchen and the landing, while her own bedroom was decidedly feminine with cream duvet and curtains and a brass bed-head.

Paul's room was painted dark blue, the walls inevitably covered with posters of motorbikes and sporting events. A black and red striped duvet covered the bed, his hi-fi, books and sports gear filled the shelves and on the desk beneath the window stood his computer—a present from Fee on his sixteenth birthday.

In the sitting-room Nadine sank down onto the sofa, kicked off her shoes, leaned her head back and relaxed. It hadn't been a particularly easy day, if she was honest, and when she really thought about it that was mainly because of the presence of the new registrar. She hadn't been joking when she'd told her mother that she could see trouble ahead; she really did have the feeling that there was going to be trouble in some form or another on her ward.

Wearily she closed her eyes. She wouldn't think about it now. She would relax, just for a few minutes, then she would take a shower, before cooking supper. Later she and Paul would go to the sports centre for a leisurely swim. Time enough tomorrow to worry about work, and trouble...trouble in the form of an Italian registrar called Angelo Fabrielli.

The sports centre was Hawksford's latest pride and joy, the large glass-domed building dominating the skyline alongside the Spencer Rathbone Memorial Hospital. The facilities, as well as two large indoor swimming-pools, included squash courts, a sauna and jacuzzi, a restaurant and bar, a multi-gym and badminton and tennis courts. The facilities were well attended at all times, and that evening when Nadine and Paul arrived seemed to be no exception.

They were both strong swimmers and, after emerging

from the changing-rooms and entering the water, they completed several laps of the pool. Then Nadine, leaving Paul to exert his superiority and swim a few more lengths, swam to the poolside and, treading water, smoothed her hair back from her face.

After watching Paul for a time and relaxing in the warm water, Nadine swam to the steps and climbed out of the pool, standing for a moment at the side still watching her son as he streaked through the water.

It was then, as she stood there dripping water, that she had the uncanny sensation of being watched. She looked around her but the poolside was clear, then something made her look up—up into the bar, whose windows overlooked the pool.

She saw her watcher immediately—saw and recognised him as he stood there, looking down at her. As their eyes met he inclined his head in acknowledgement.

Nadine nodded curtly in response and then, suddenly embarrassed, she grabbed her towel from the poolside rail where she had left it and wrapped it around her, covering her black swimsuit and as much of her body as she could.

What in the world was he doing here? she thought angrily. Hadn't she had enough of him that day at work, without him encroaching on her precious leisure time?

Turning away sharply, she managed to catch Paul's eye and indicated that she was going to the changing-rooms. He flicked the water from his eyes, then gave her a thumbs-up sign.

By the time Nadine had showered, dried her hair, put on her jeans, shirt and navy jumper and left the changing-rooms, there was no sign of Paul. She knew that he changed much faster than she did and that usually he sat outside on the wall waiting for her.

As she walked through the foyer she threw a quick glance in the direction of the bar, but mercifully there was now no sign of Angelo Fabrielli.

When she stepped outside, however, her relief was short-lived because at first she couldn't see Paul either, then eventually she caught sight of him some distance away. Hoisting her sports bag onto her shoulder, Nadine made her way towards Paul, wondering as she did so why he was in that particular section of the car park when she had parked their car on the other side.

It wasn't until she drew closer that she had her answer. Paul was prowling around something which was hidden from Nadine's view by a high-sided transit van but, from the look of awe and admiration on her son's face, as she approached some sixth sense told her exactly what she was about to see.

'Isn't it fantastic?' Paul said, without looking up, as she came and stood beside him.

She nodded. 'Yes,' she agreed grudgingly, 'it is pretty impressive.'

'Do you think it's the one you. . .?' Paul began eagerly, but was cut short by a voice that broke into his question.

'I thought it was you. I see you in the water and I think, yes, it is Sister Hadley, although she looks very different from when I last see her.'

Paul spun round, but Nadine turned more slowly. 'Dr Fabrielli,' she said coolly. 'Today seems to be full of surprises, doesn't it?'

'It certainly does.' He paused and looked at Paul. Just for one moment Nadine could see the puzzlement in his eyes—a puzzlement she had seen many times before when people tried to work out her relationship to the boy.

'I was just saying what a fantastic bike this is,' said Paul.

'Ah, you like it?' Dr Fabrielli laughed, his teeth very white against his olive complexion. 'She rides like a dream.'

Paul glanced at Nadine, and she supposed she ought to say something. 'Paul,' she took a deep breath, 'this is my colleague, Dr Fabrielli.' She turned her head slightly and as Paul stepped forward, hand outstretched, she completed the introduction by saying, 'Dr Fabrielli—my son, Paul.'

She saw his dark eyes widen; saw the surprise flicker in their depths as he shook Paul's hand. 'Surely not,' he murmured. 'Your son? But how is this possible?' He turned his head to look at Nadine. 'You cannot be old enough.'

Paul, bored by the type of comments he had heard many times before, turned his attention back to the bike so it was only Nadine who saw Angelo Fabrielli's puzzled gaze fly to her left hand. He recovered quickly, she granted him that, as, with a slightly bemused smile, he too turned back to the bike and to Paul.

'So you like motorbikes, Paul?' he said.

'Oh, yes,' Paul breathed reverently and then, glancing back at Nadine, he grinned and added, 'Much to Mum's disgust! She thinks that it's inevitable that everyone who has a motorbike will automatically have an accident.'

'Ah, it's not the bike, it's the person riding it. . .'

'That's what I said!' Paul flashed his mother a triumphant look. 'See, Mother, even Dr Fabrielli agrees with me.'

'Please, all my friends at home in Italy call me Angelo—you must too. Dr Fabrielli is. . .is too formal.' Looking from one to the other, he spread his hands.

'OK,' said Paul, turning back to the bike yet again.

'How old are you, Paul?' asked Angelo.

Nadine threw him a sharp glance. She had the feeling that there was an ulterior motive to his asking, like trying to work out how old she was.

'Sixteen,' replied Paul, without looking up. By this time he was crouched down beside the bike.

'A little young yet,' mused Angelo. 'I was eighteen before I had my first bike.'

Paul's face fell.

'Although,' Angelo paused and again came the devastating smile, 'I have to confess, before that I have a scooter. . .'

'There you are, you see. . .' said Paul to Nadine half-accusingly. 'I could have something small to start with.'

'It is. . .' Angelo shrugged '. . .how you say. . .com-pulsory in Rome. . . Everyone has scooter. . . It is the only way. . .the traffic is. . .' he gave a hopeless—almost comical—gesture, leaving the sentence unfinished. Then, looking lovingly at the bike, he said, 'Perhaps you like a ride on this?'

Nadine stiffened.

'A ride. . .?' Paul's voice, at times unpredictable since it broke, squeaked embarrassingly.

'Yes, on the bike.' Angelo nodded.

'What—now?' Paul's voice was deep again.

'Why not?' Angelo shrugged. 'I take you home.'

Paul glanced quickly at Nadine, his glance implying an expected objection from her. Suddenly she realised that Angelo Fabrielli also was looking at her. She wanted to object. Wanted to refuse on Paul's behalf. But how could she? It would embarrass him terribly, giving the impression that at sixteen he still needed her permission for everything he wanted to do. In the end she said hopefully, 'But you don't have a crash helmet.'

She might have known that Angelo Fabrielli would carry a spare helmet in one of those pannier things on the side of the black monster. In the time it took him to walk to the back of the bike and produce the helmet, Nadine knew that Paul would get his wish.

It wasn't that she wanted to curtail his fun, she thought as she watched while both he and Angelo secured their helmets, it was simply that she had an innate fear and distrust of motorbikes, born, no doubt, from her long association with the victims of so many road accidents involving the machines. That, and the fact that it was Angelo Fabrielli who was taking him. Why that should matter she wasn't really sure, except that the new registrar seemed to have been a scource of irritation since the moment she had met him.

She watched as first Angelo, then Paul, mounted the machine.

'I'll see you at home, Mum,' said Paul. In the split second before he pulled down the helmet's visor Nadine noticed that his eyes were shining with excitement, then he leaned forward and, above the noise of the engine, shouted to Angelo, 'I'll direct you.'

'I think I know where you live.' Angelo's reply was accompanied by a wink in Nadine's direction, before he too adjusted his visor. Then they were gone—down the hill to the main road.

Nadine watched them go and when the sound of the Harley Davidson's engine was little more than an echo she turned and walked slowly across the car park to where she had left her car.

It was quite dark by the time she drove down the steep hill into Hawksford's town centre but the streetlights, together with the shop windows and the motorway lights beyond the town, lit the night sky until it was almost as bright as day.

The outline of Hawksford's medieval castle rose sharply on one side of the road, its ramparts illuminated by floodlights, and when at last Nadine drew into the quiet, tree-lined avenue where she lived, above her on the hill, she could see quite clearly the lighted buildings of the Spencer Rathbone Hospital and the sports centre.

To Nadine's relief there was no sign of the motorbike in the road, but as she drew into the gateway of Montague House and parked behind Fee's green Fiesta she saw with a stab of annoyance that the bike was parked on the other side of the drive.

Surely Paul hadn't asked him in? But would that be so surprising? Wasn't that exactly what she would expect her son to do? Wasn't that part of the pattern of good manners that she had taken such pains to instil into him? It would have come totally naturally to Paul to have invited Angelo Fabrielli into the house, especially after his having just given him a lift home.

Nadine switched off the engine and sat for a moment, without attempting to get out of the car. She had seen the excitement in her son's eyes, and that had been before his ride—there was no telling what he would be like now.

With a sigh she at last released her seat belt, opened the car door and got out. The house was in darkness, save for the light from the hall that shone through the stained-glass fanlight above the front door. As she passed her mother's car it occurred to Nadine that Fee had returned earlier than usual from her rehearsal, then the thought was gone for, as she opened the front door, she was confronted by the sound of laughter.

Slowly she walked down the hall and pushed open the kitchen door.

They were all three sitting round the kitchen table— Fee, Paul and Angelo Fabrielli. Between them stood a bottle of Chianti and, on Fee's little Japanese enamel tray, four empty glasses.

They all turned to look at Nadine and for one moment there was silence, then they all started to talk at once.

'Here she is.' That was Angelo.

'Good, now we can pour the wine.' Her mother.

'Mum, it was brilliant!' That was Paul.

Nadine continued to stand in the open doorway. She had half expected to find that Fee would have made coffee, or even tea—but wine?

Almost as if she could read her thoughts, Fee said, 'I opened the Chianti, Nadine—I had to when I knew our guest was Italian.' She said it almost apologetically as if she half feared Nadine's reaction.

Guest? Nadine frowned. He'd only brought Paul home from the sports centre, for goodness' sake! That hardly made him a guest. She stared at him as laughingly he stopped Fee from pouring too much wine into his glass.

'I still have to drive, after all,' he said.

'Of course,' Fee smiled back at him, then looked at
Nadine again with the bottle poised in her hand. 'You
will have some, won't you, darling?'

Nadine half inclined her head. 'You're home early
tonight,' she said, for something to say, rather than
feeling obliged to meet those disturbing dark eyes
again.

Fee laughed. 'The rehearsal was terrible—just about
as bad as it could possibly be. The director sent us all
home in disgust, but—' she shrugged and looked at
Angelo '—not to worry—we have a saying here that
everything will be all right on the night.'

'Of course.' Angelo laughed too. 'Then you
celebrate. . .yes?'

'Yes, then we celebrate.' Fee poured more wine and
handed Nadine a glass.

'I was just thinking that this has a celebratory air
about it,' remarked Nadine, glancing round the table
and at the same time wishing that Angelo would stop
looking at her.

'Well, I suppose, really, that's just what it is,' replied
Fee, '—a celebration.'

'What do you mean?' Nadine looked quickly from
one to the other. 'Is there something I'm missing here?'

'Well,' said Fee, 'it's not every day we find a new
lodger, is it?'

Carefully Nadine set her glass down on the table and
stared at her mother. 'What do you mean?' she said
quietly.

'Dr Fabrielli,' said Fee happily, 'Angelo, I mean—'
she flashed him a smile, and he in turn inclined his head
in response '—was just telling us that he is to look for
new lodgings as the ones he is in at the moment are
totally unsatisfactory. So I told him that we usually
have a lodger, and we've had people from the hospital
before—prefer them, in fact—and at the moment our

spare room is empty, so I said we would be only too happy for him to come and stay with us.' She turned to Nadine. 'Wouldn't we, dear?' she added.

CHAPTER THREE

'BUT what on earth possessed you to offer him a room?'
Nadine stared at her mother across the kitchen table. It
was an hour later; Angelo had left and Paul had gone
to his room. 'You'd only met him ten minutes earlier,
for heaven's sake!'

'I know, darling,' said Fee, 'and all I did was ask
where he was living.'

'So, what did he say to that?' demanded Nadine. She
was feeling tense and upset by the events of the evening.

'He said he was in hospital accommodation, but that
he would be looking for something more satisfactory.'

'I would have thought he would be looking for his
own flat. . .'

'He said he won't be in this country long enough for
that, but he prefers to be with other people; he doesn't
like living alone.'

'So what was wrong with the hospital accommodation? There are plenty of people around there,' snapped
Nadine.

'Ah, but he meant a family,' said Fee seriously. 'He
is Italian, don't forget. . .'

'As if I could,' muttered Nadine.

'And I read somewhere once that in Italy the family
is all-important. Do you know, as soon as I mentioned
that we take lodgers and that our spare room was empty
he jumped at it?'

'I bet he did,' retorted Nadine. 'He probably envisages
you doing all his cooking and laundry.'

'Oh, I don't think so, dear. . . In fact. . .'

'Well, let's face it, Mother, he certainly didn't waste
any time in getting his feet under the table, did he?'

36

'I thought you would be pleased. . .' Fee trailed off miserably.

'Pleased?'

'Well, you were only saying the other day that it was time we got another lodger. . .'

'Only because you were saying it was getting more and more difficult to make ends meet!'

'In the past you've always been pleased if we were able to get someone from the hospital. . . You said it made for a good reference. . .that it was far better than allowing a total stranger into the house.'

'I know I did,' muttered Nadine. 'But. . .but not him!'

'What's wrong with him?' Fee stared helplessly at her. 'Honestly, Nadine, I simply don't understand you sometimes. I thought he was a perfectly charming young man and Paul quite obviously liked him as well, which surely is a bonus.'

'He'll be trouble. I just know it,' said Nadine shaking her head.

'But why? How do you know that? You've only just met him yourself. It's not because he's Italian, is it?' Fee narrowed her eyes and peered suspiciously at Nadine.

'Of course not.'

'I didn't think it could be that. . .so what is it, then?'

Nadine gave a deep sigh and sank down onto a chair. 'I'm not really sure. I suppose I'm being unfair. But it's just that in the short time he's been on Ortho he seems to have caused havoc amongst the staff.'

'Because he's young, Italian and handsome?' Fee raised one eyebrow. 'You can hardly blame him for that, Nadine. Surely, if anyone's at fault it's your nurses for being susceptible to his charm.'

'Isn't that precisely what's just happened to you?'

'Not at all,' replied Fee with uncharacteristic crispness. 'I'm simply being practical.'

Nadine still had difficulty in accepting what had happened, and this wasn't helped by Paul's enthusing the following morning about how he would be able to have

more rides on the Harley Davidson if Angelo was actually living in the house. In the end she was glad to leave
for work, while at the same time she knew that when
she got there she would be faced with a similar situation
and the same cause for her irritation.

This morning, however, her parking space was empty
and there was no sign of the motorbike or its rider. For
the moment she forgot about Angelo Fabrielli and it
was not until after she had changed into her uniform,
taken report from the night staff and was discussing
patient care with Jayne and Ruth, that she was reminded
of him again. To her surprise, she heard the sound of
the registrar's unmistakable Italian accent coming from
the ward.

'Surely it's not doctors' round already?' She glanced
at her fob watch then looked sharply from Jayne to Ruth,
noticing as she did so that Ruth's cheeks had grown
quite pink.

Jayne shook her head. 'No,' she said, 'he must have
just called in to see someone.'

'I think,' said Nadine, 'I'll take a wander down the
ward and see just who that someone is.'

'Well, it can't be Lee,' Jayne chuckled, '—she's not
on duty until later.'

'I know,' replied Nadine grimly, 'that's what's con-
cerning me. Who he's chatting up this time.'

Purposefully she strode off down the ward, only to
find the new registrar talking quietly to Cyril Norman.
He looked up as she approached, his expression softening as his eyes met hers.

'Here is Sister now,' he said to Cyril, who was looking
decidedly frail after his operation.

'Good morning, Mr Norman.' Nadine smiled and,
glancing at Angelo, she said, 'Do we have a problem?'

'No, no problem.' He too smiled but he volunteered
no further explanation for his presence on the ward so
early in the morning.

'I just wondered,' said Nadine. 'It's not often we have

the honour of a registrar's attention at such an early hour...'

'Unless there is some sort of problem...' Angelo laughed. 'No, Sister, I am simply here to fulfil a promise, that is all,' he glanced at Cyril as he spoke.

'A promise?' Nadine frowned. Why was nothing straightforward with this man?

'Yes,' he nodded. 'Yesterday, I see Cyril's wife. She was very worried about him. Cyril was still sleepy from his anaesthetic. I told her, "Tomorrow morning I will come to see your husband..."' he trailed off with a shrug.

'Just to make sure we are looking after him properly?' asked Nadine coolly. For a moment she had the satisfaction of seeing Angelo look a little uncomfortable, then the moment was gone and he laughed his lazy, easy laugh.

'I know you look after him well,' he said in his slightly broken English. 'I shall tell Mrs Norman, "If your Cyril is on Sister Hadley's ward, he have the best care in the hospital."'

'Flattery will get you nowhere, Dr Fabrielli,' replied Nadine crisply then, looking at Cyril over the top of her reading glasses which she had been wearing in the office and had forgotten to remove, she said, 'I trust you are being well looked after, Mr Norman?'

'Yes, yes, thank you, Sister,' replied Cyril, peering at them both in turn through his thick-lensed spectacles and, as Nadine would have turned to go he added, 'Although, I was just saying to the doc here, I could do with another slice of toast.'

'I'll see that you get one,' said Nadine.

'And I'll see you later, Cyril,' said Angelo, 'during doctors' round when Mr Russell comes to see you.'

Cyril nodded, obviously contented with the treatment he was receiving, while Nadine, together with the registrar, moved away from his bed.

'You did not mind me coming into the ward?' asked

Angelo. He sounded anxious and just for a moment
Nadine felt guilty that she might have embarrassed him
in front of a patient when his objective had apparently
only been an act of compassion.

'No,' she said, 'no, of course not. It's unusual, that's
all. I assumed there must be some sort of problem and,
as the night report on Mr Norman had been satisfactory,
I wondered what could be wrong.'

'Sometimes,' Angelo sighed, 'sometimes I don't
understand your rules; sometimes they are very different
from what I am used to in Italy. It was just that Mrs
Norman. . .she seemed so. . .upset and I wanted to make
her feel better. . .so I promise. . .' he shrugged helplessly
and trailed off, 'I get things wrong. . .I am sorry. . .I will
go now.'

Suddenly Nadine felt sorry for him, in spite of the
fact that he seemed to be the cause for so much irritation.
The misunderstandings which had occurred—the space
in the car park, which hadn't been marked when all
was said and done, and now the unwritten law of ward
procedure—were both things which would appear con-
fusing to a foreigner and which, when examined, were
really downright petty.

She took a deep breath. 'Not so fast,' she said, and
he paused and looked questioningly at her. 'Now that
you are here, Dr Fabrielli, maybe you would have a
look at another patient?'

'But of course,' he said, as if only too anxious to
make amends, then he added quickly, 'on one condition.'

Nadine stiffened. 'Condition?' She threw him a quick
glance, saw the amusement lurking in the dark eyes, and
wondered what she might be about to hear next.

'Yes,' he replied smoothly, 'That you call me Angelo.
After all,' he murmured, lowering his voice so that there
was no danger of anyone else overhearing, 'if we are
to live together. . .'

Nadine drew in her breath sharply. 'On the ward,'
she said, 'I shall call you Dr Fabrielli and I will require

that you address me as Sister Hadley, especially in front of my nurses. Is that clear, Doctor?'

'Of course,' he said, 'quite clear, Sister. But what about at home?' he added softly. By this time they had reached the double swing doors at the top of the men's section of the ward.

'What do you mean, "at home"?' Nadine almost snapped, annoyed now by his air of familiarity.

'Well,' he answered patiently, 'I take it there I shall be permitted to call you Nadine?'

For the moment Nadine could think of no suitable reply. She wanted to tell him there and then that it was nothing to do with her that he was going to be lodging at her home; that it had been all her mother's doing, and that if it had been down to her she would almost certainly have said no. But she couldn't say that. To do so would sound rude and could possibly be misconstrued, especially to a fellow colleague and one from overseas at that.

If she was strictly honest she wasn't really sure why she was so against the idea and, come to that, why she was so irritated by this handsome, charming stranger at all. Maybe it was simply that—the fact that he *was* so handsome and charming. Maybe she was getting old and cynical, she told herself.

But, whatever it was, she found herself biting her tongue, as she refrained from the type of comment she might have made. Instead, she ignored his question and led the way into the ladies' section of the ward to the bed of a patient who had received a new hip joint the previous day.

'This is Peggy Simpkins, Doctor,' she said, taking the chart from the foot of the bed and handing it to him. 'She had her hip replacement yesterday, and she is suffering quite a lot of discomfort this morning, isn't that so, Peggy?'

The patient, who was in her sixties, nodded and

Angelo smiled at her then studied her chart. 'Is it the pain, Peggy?' he asked sympathetically.

'Not so much the pain, Doctor,' replied Peggy grimly, 'I can cope with that. It's this wretched wedge.'

As Peggy spoke, Nadine lifted back the bedcover to reveal a large piece of foam rubber between her legs.

'I didn't get a wink of sleep all night,' Peggy grumbled. 'Honestly, it's the most uncomfortable thing you could imagine. Can't you take it away?' She addressed Nadine, who in turn glanced at Angelo. 'Oh, I know it's to stop me crossing my legs,' said Peggy when neither of them spoke, 'but if I promise not to. . .? Honestly, I feel as if my back is breaking.'

'Could we not take it away, Sister?' asked Angelo. 'If Peggy promises?'

'It's one of the hardest things in the world not to cross one's ankles whilst lying in bed,' said Nadine.

'Well, maybe a pillow would be more comfortable. . .?'

'If you say so, Doctor,' replied Nadine.

'We'll try it,' said Angelo, earning himself a smile of relieved gratitude from the patient, 'and I think we should look at pain control and possibly increase it for a while. . . Have you been out of bed yet, Peggy, for a walk?'

'Oh, no!' Peggy looked horrified.

'You've got that delight to come, haven't you, Peggy?' Nadine smiled, then gently she added, 'Don't worry, it's not nearly so bad as it sounds. . .you'll be amazed.'

Together they left Peggy's bed and walked back to the nurses' station. 'Was that all?' asked Angelo.

Nadine shook her head.

'I didn't think it could be,' he murmured.

'Peggy is also on Metoprolol for hypertension, which I feel may need adjustment. You saw her blood pressure readings on her chart?'

He nodded. 'Yes, I noticed. Shall we go to your office and talk about her medication?'

They turned and were about to enter Nadine's office when Barry Fletcher suddenly called out from his bed.

'How are the rehearsals going, Sister?' he said

'Not terribly well last night, according to my mother,' replied Nadine.

'I wish I was with them,' said Barry enviously. 'Do you know this will be the first production I've missed since the company was formed. . .and it had to be *The Gondoliers*, didn't it? That's always been my favourite.'

'Never mind, Barry,' Nadine replied, conscious as she did so of Angelo's interested expression. 'You'll be there for the next one.'

'What is this. . .this Gondoliers?' asked Angelo, mystified, as Nadine closed her office door behind them.

'It's the performance that the local operatic company is producing,' she replied.

'This is what your mother is part of?'

Nadine nodded, 'Yes, she is a great enthusiast of operetta, just as Barry Fletcher is. He's devastated that he has to miss this production.'

'I don't really understand this. . .this operetta,' mused Angelo. 'In my country we have grand opera. . .'

'I think that might be a little beyond the Hawksford Amateur Operatic Company,' smiled Nadine then, growing serious, she said, 'You like opera?'

Angelo nodded, then shrugged. 'I grow up with it. My family. . .in Rome we always attend the opera. . . but I also like rock, I like heavy metal, I like jazz. . .I like. . .'

'I get the picture. . .you like music.' Nadine laughed.

'Yes,' he, too, laughed, 'I like music,' then, as if quick to seize the lightening of the atmosphere, he said, 'I like your mother too; she is kind and it is good of her to say I can be your new lodger. . .and the room, it is very good.'

'Yes, well. . .' For a moment Nadine, caught off

guard, was lost for words then, as she searched desperately for something to say, Angelo carried on speaking.

'I still find it hard to believe Paul is your son. You really don't look old enough to have a son of this age.'

'Well, I can assure you Paul is my son. . .' she said lightly, 'although I must confess I was very young when I had him. . .' She trailed off as she saw the renewed interest in Angelo's eyes. The last thing she had intended was to get into a conversation of this nature with him.

'He is so dark, while you are so fair. . .' his gaze roamed over her face and her hair, most of which was tucked out of sight beneath the white frilled sister's cap she wore, '. . .but maybe his father was dark. . .'

'Yes,' she nodded, 'his father was dark.' Briskly she moved to her desk and picked up the patient's medication chart. 'This won't do, Doctor,' she said. 'I have work to do, just as I'm sure you have. So, if you'll just have a look at Peggy's medication. . .'

'Of course,' he replied then, just as he'd made the necessary dose adjustments, there came a knock at the office door and he looked up.

When the door was pushed open Karen Ashton, one of the orthopaedic unit's health support workers, appeared. She glanced from Nadine to Angelo, her expression unmistakably softening as she saw the doctor.

Nadine, remembering that Karen was one of the girls supposedly attracted to the new registrar, found herself being more brisk than she might have been. 'What can I do for you, Karen?' she asked, taking note of the girl's suddenly bright eyes and slightly flushed cheeks.

'We are about to change Josh's dressings,' Karen replied. 'You said you wanted to see the wound this time, Nadine.'

'Yes, I did. Thank you, Karen, I'll be right there.' She glanced at Angelo. 'If you'll excuse me, Dr Fabrielli.'

'Of course,' Angelo replied. 'I must go anyway; Mr

Russell will think I have. . .how you say it. . .done
a bunk?'

Karen laughed, flicking back her auburn hair, and
even Nadine found herself smiling, and as Angelo
passed Karen in the doorway he said, 'You not forget
our game of squash tonight?'

'Oh, no,' breathed Karen. Then, as Angelo disappeared into the corridor after a backward glance and
another devastating smile at the two women, she said,
'Isn't he absolutely gorgeous?'

'Just don't go getting too carried away,' replied
Nadine drily. 'You know the reputation these Latin
types have.'

'I know,' sighed Karen, 'but he is gorgeous, you have
to admit that. And he's asked me out. . . You heard what
he said—we're having a game of squash tonight, and
we're bound to go for a drink afterwards.'

'That's fine,' replied Nadine, wondering if the girl
knew that the registrar had also apparently taken Lee
Bevan out as well, 'but just watch your step, Karen,
that's all I'm saying.'

'He could be enough to make a girl leave home,' said
Karen dreamily then, when she caught sight of Nadine's
expression, she added, 'Oh, come on, Nadine, he really
is gorgeous—surely even you have to admit that?'

'You mean, even an oldie like me?' Nadine laughed
when Karen looked embarrassed by what she might have
implied, and she added somewhat grudgingly, 'Well,
he's certainly very good-looking, but I'm not sure he
would be my type. . .'

'Oh. . .?' Karen sounded amazed, as if she found it
incredible that any woman would not immediately suc-
cumb to that particular brand of charm and looks.

'For a start, he's much too young. . .' protested
Nadine.

'Oh, I don't know. . .' Karen said quickly, as if to
make amends for her earlier implication.

'Oh, come on, he's years younger than me,' said

Nadine. 'If I went after someone like that I would be accused of cradle-snatching.'

'I don't see why,' Karen shrugged. 'Lots of women go for younger men, especially these days, and besides—' she peered at Nadine '—I wouldn't have said you were that much older than him. But what am I saying?' She grinned suddenly. 'I'm glad you're not interested—you'd only increase the competition if you were!'

Nadine laughed. 'What you're saying is us oldies should stick to our own age group and leave the way clear for you youngsters—is that it?'

It was Karen's turn to laugh. 'If that's the case then someone should have a word with Ruth.'

'Ruth?' Nadine had turned back to her desk but she paused and looked curiously at the younger girl.

'Yes, she's definitely after Angelo Fabrielli.'

'Oh, come on, Karen,' she protested. 'Ruth might find him attractive, but I can't believe she's actually after him.'

'Then what's she doing putting blonde streaks in her hair?' demanded Karen. 'If that's not trying to attract his attention, I don't know what is. . . Not that it'll work. Angelo wouldn't look twice at Ruth—now, she really is too old for him.'

'Ruth's not that much older than me,' said Nadine, lowering her voice as they moved out of the office into the ward.

'Isn't she?' Karen sounded genuinely surprised. 'I would have said she was years older than you.'

Nadine became caught up in the busy flurry of the ward's morning routine, and she had no further time to give a thought to Angelo Fabrielli or the love lives of her members of staff.

She supervised the changing of Josh Barnes's dressings and decided that she wanted Mr Russell to examine the wound at the top of the boy's thigh, as it appeared red and angry and was oozing pus.

'What's wrong, Sister?' Fear flickered in Josh's eyes as he looked up at her.

'A bit of infection around the wound, Josh,' she replied lightly.

'Is it serious?'

'It happens sometimes,' she answered casually.

'But what does it mean?' Josh persisted.

'Let's wait and see what Mr Russell says, shall we?' said Nadine kindly, glancing first at her watch then at Karen and Jayne Reynolds who were attending to Josh that morning. 'The doctors should be round soon,' she said, 'so just cover the wound with a light dressing for the time being.'

Leaving Josh with the two nurses, she crossed the ward to Barry Fletcher—who was still lying flat on his back. He had his Walkman over his head and his eyes were closed as he listened to the music so he was unaware of Nadine's presence until she touched his wrist lightly, then his eyes snapped open.

'Oh, hello, Sister,' he grinned, and adjusted the control on the Walkman. 'Didn't know you were there.'

'How are you this morning, Barry?' she asked.

'Fantastic!' he grinned.

'Any problems?'

'None at all. Not unless you count climbing the walls as a problem.'

'It will come to an end, Barry,' she said quietly, 'I promise you. You are over halfway now—you just have to hang on in there.'

'Yes, I know,' he sighed and, moving his head slightly, he looked across the ward to Josh. 'I'm lucky, compared to that poor little blighter over there; he had a bad night again, you know, Sister.'

'I know he did, Barry,' Nadine replied.

'Must have been in a lot of pain; kept calling for his mum, he did.'

'The doctor's coming to see him soon—we'll try and

sort out the pain he's having. Now, while we're on the subject of pain, Barry, what about yours?'

'Oh, I can cope,' Barry grinned. 'When it gets too bad I imagine having a tooth out without anaesthetic— I soon forget my pain then.'

'Well, that's a new one on me, I must say.' Nadine laughed.

'Funny thing is,' Barry went on, 'I seem to have as much pain in my hip as in my back.'

'That's not unusual after a fusion,' said Nadine. 'Don't forget, the bone that has been grafted into your spine has actually been taken from your hip. It's bound to be sore for a time.'

Leaving Barry to think about what she'd just said, she moved on to Cyril Norman's bed. The *Daily Mail* lay open on the bedcovers and Cyril had fallen asleep, his glasses tilted at an angle across his face. Nadine looked down at him for a moment then, leaning forward, gently removed his glasses and placed them on top of his locker.

When she reached the end of the ward she glanced back, checking that all was in order for the doctors' round. Bright sunshine streamed through the windows, highlighting the splashes of colour from the spring flowers on the window-sills and bedside lockers. The beds had all been neatly remade, the ward cleaned and the patients bathed or washed—depending on their particular stage of treatment.

Nadine felt a little surge of satisfaction as she surveyed her domain. She had fought long and hard to attain her present position and status and she took great pride in the ward, the patients and the staff in her care. Her moment of self-congratulation was short-lived, however, for at that moment, through the circle of clear glass on one of the swing doors, she caught sight of Seymour Russell's tall, slightly stooped figure and she realised that the morning's round was about to start.

Somehow she carefully managed to avoid eye contact

with Angelo Farbrielli as she conducted the doctors around the ward. If she'd been asked why she did so, she would have been hard-pushed to give a rational explanation. What she did know was that, in spite of not looking at him, she was only too aware of his presence within the group—uncomfortably so.

Josh Barnes received the most attention that morning as Seymour Russell carefully examined the wound, which was showing increasing signs of infection.

'Looks as if we might have a bit of a problem here, Josh,' the consultant said at last as he straightened up.

'So what's going to happen?' Josh looked really worried now, his face pale and drawn from the pain he was suffering.

'Well, you know you have a pin in this leg?' said Seymour Russell, and when Josh nodded he went on, 'It looks as if it's become rather infected. I think what we need to do, therefore, is to whip you back down to Theatre so that we can have another look and see what's going on.'

'You mean another operation?' There was no mistaking the dismay in Josh's voice.

'I'm afraid so,' replied Seymour. 'We may need to replace the pin. Don't worry, though, it's quite straightforward. Really nothing at all to worry about.' He looked over his shoulder. 'Ah, Dr Fabrielli,' he said, his gaze seeking and then coming to rest on Angelo, 'one for you to assist with, I would say. Quite appropriate, really—one motorcycle fanatic to another.'

He gave a short bark of a laugh, which was accompanied by polite smiles from the rest of his team, then while Josh remained wide-eyed and unsmiling, gazing from one to the other, Seymour Russell peered over his glasses at Nadine. 'After lunch, I should think, Sister— this young man for Theatre, if you'll prepare, please. And I should like a course of antibiotics started immediately, if you'll write him up please, Dr Fabrielli. And his analgesics—now let me see, what has he been taking?'

'Co-proxamol,' said Nadine, consulting Josh's chart, 'but he's been in a lot of pain.'

'In that case I think we should change to dihydrocodeine—just until this present crisis is over. Now, who's next?' With a rather absent-minded nod at Josh, Seymour Russell moved on to the next bed.

When the doctors' round was complete and the team had left the ward Nadine immediately returned to Josh and drew the curtains around his bed.

'Come on, Josh, cheer up,' she said briskly. 'It isn't the end of the world, you know.'

'I know,' he replied, biting his lip and at the same time fighting back his tears. 'It's just that I thought all that was over—Theatre and operations and all that stuff. I suppose I'll be sick again all day tomorrow.'

'Not necessarily,' Nadine replied, and then, as she straightened his bedclothes, she saw through the crack in the curtains that Angelo had come back into the ward, and was talking to Ruth. Did the man never stop chatting up the staff? she thought with a stab of annoyance. She really would have to have a word with him; she simply couldn't have him keep disrupting her staff in this way.

'I was last time,' said Josh.

'You were what?' She looked down at Josh, wondering for a moment what he was talking about—so distracted had she been by the reappearance of the registrar on the ward.

'Sick,' Josh replied.

'Maybe you won't need a general anaesthetic this time,' said Nadine, still with one eye on the crack between the curtains. 'I'll have a word with the anaesthetist for you.'

'Do you mean Dr Fabrielli?'

'No,' said Nadine abruptly, 'he's a registrar, not an anaesthetist.'

'Is he really a motorbike fanatic?' Josh suddenly grinned, in spite of his pain.

'You'd better ask him that for yourself,' replied

Nadine. 'Now, Josh, I want you to lie quietly for a while
and rest, then Karen will come and get you ready for
Theatre. And you really mustn't worry, you know—
we'll soon have you right again.'

Stepping out of the cubicle, Nadine twitched the curtains closed behind her, and as she approached Angelo
and Ruth they both turned to look at her.

'Distracting my nurses again, Dr Fabrielli?' Nadine
raised her eyebrows.

'Ah, if only. . .' Angelo sighed and smiled at Ruth,
the look implying that he wished it was in his power to
distract her. Ruth flushed and Nadine frowned, then
Angelo grew serious. 'Actually,' he said, 'I came back
to talk to our young friend.' He nodded towards Josh's
curtained-off bed. 'I wonder. . . A chat about motorbikes
might help to relax him. . . What do you think, Sister
Hadley?'

Nadine's breath caught in her throat. Why was it that
this man always seemed to have the power to catch
her out? 'What do you think, Dr Fabrielli,' she said,
'considering it was a motorbike that put him where he
is today?'

'I'd still like to try,' he replied. 'With your permission, of course, Sister?'

'How can I refuse, Dr Fabrielli?' she said. She made
to move away to return to her office when Angelo, who
had begun to walk towards Josh's bed, suddenly stopped
and looked back over his shoulder.

'There was one other thing while I'm here, Sister
Hadley,' he said.

There must have been something in his tone of voice
which implied that what he was about to say was in
some way out of the ordinary because not only did
Nadine stop and look back but Ruth, who had been
about to enter the sluice, also paused to listen.

'You've given me your permission to speak to Josh,'
said Angelo, and there was no mistaking the amusement
in his eyes as he spoke. 'Now that we've agreed that I

shall be living with you, do I also have your permission to move in this evening—or is that perhaps a little too soon?'

CHAPTER FOUR

NADINE stiffened, for a moment uncertain whether Angelo was being deliberately audacious or whether his request was genuinely innocent and devoid of innuendo. Whichever it was, she was only too aware of Ruth's incredulous look but somehow she managed to pull herself together. 'Not at all, Dr Fabrielli,' she heard herself reply smoothly. 'When exactly this evening did you have in mind—before your game of squash with Karen Ashton, or after?'

If she had intended to disarm him in any way by the mention of his date with Karen she was unsuccessful. 'Oh, after,' he replied without any hesitation. 'My game of squash is straight after my shift.'

He went then, to Nadine's relief, to talk to Josh, but she was left with Ruth's indignant curiosity.

'What in the world was he talking about?' Ruth followed her into the office and stared at Nadine, her pale eyelashes twitching. 'Moving in with you? What did he mean?'

Nadine took a deep breath. 'My mother has invited Dr Fabrielli to be our new lodger.'

Ruth's jaw dropped in amazement. 'Well,' she said when she had recovered a little, 'I must say you haven't wasted any time.'

'We usually have a lodger.' Nadine found herself trying to explain, not wanting Ruth to get the wrong impression. 'The last one went a couple of months ago and the room has been empty since then. Apparently Dr Fabrielli was unhappy with his present accommodation so my mother—'

'But how does your mother know him?'

'She doesn't know him.' Nadine shook her head. 'At

53

least, she didn't, not until last night that is. . .when he came to the house.'

'Came to the house?' Ruth frowned.

'That's what I said,' replied Nadine and then, her exasperation growing, she added, 'What is this Ruth, the third degree?'

'No, no of course not,' Ruth mumbled, and had the grace to look shamefaced. 'Dr Fabrielli hasn't been in this country for long and I just wondered how your mother knew him, that's all.'

Suddenly Nadine felt sorry for her. It really did seem as if Ruth was smitten with the young registrar, something entirely out of character for usually she kept herself to herself and led a very quiet, uneventful sort of existence. 'He came to the house, Ruth,' she said, but more gently this time, 'because he gave my son, Paul, a lift home from the sports centre on his motorbike.'

'Oh, oh, I see,' mumbled Ruth, lowering her gaze.

'Paul asked him in,' Nadine went on, 'and my mother, being my mother, provided hospitality. Before I even arrived on the scene she had offered him the spare room as well.'

Ruth looked quite taken aback, as if she really didn't know what to say next.

'Now,' said Nadine firmly, but not unkindly, 'do you think we could forget Dr Fabrielli and his accommodation arrangements—at least for the time being—and get on with some work?'

'Yes, of course.' Ruth appeared quite flustered by now and Nadine deliberately changed the subject.

'Would you find someone to assist you and go and help Peggy Simpkins out of bed, please, Ruth? It's high time she had a walk; she must be wondering where we've all got to.' Without another word Ruth hurried out of the office, and as Nadine looked through the open doorway she saw Karen coming out of the sluice. 'Karen. . .' she nodded towards the curtains around Josh's bed '. . .when Dr Fabrielli has finished talking, would you prepare Josh for Theatre, please? I will ring and ask the duty anaesthetist to come up and speak to him.'

The busy ward routine continued, and gradually Nadine forgot all about the fact that the new registrar would be moving into her home that evening. She wasn't reminded of it again until the end of her shift when she and Jayne were changing into their outdoor clothes.

'Any plans for tonight?' asked Jayne as she struggled into her jacket.

'Not really.' Nadine hesitated. It was on the tip of her tongue to tell Jayne what was happening in her household, but something prevented her. She had had quite enough with Ruth's reaction, without having to contend with another. She knew that it was only a matter of time before Jayne found out about her new lodger, just as everyone else would be sure to find out, but for some reason she didn't feel able to volunteer the information. Instead she found herself saying, 'Probably just a quiet night in.'

She really didn't know why she hadn't told Jayne, she thought as, a little later, she let herself into her car; after all, she had never made any secret in the past of previous lodgers. Several had been hospital employees, as Fee had pointed out the night before. Some Nadine had even become quite friendly with, sharing lifts to work or a table in the canteen, so why was she so wary about this one?

She stared at the dashboard, making no attempt to start the car. What was it about Angelo Fabrielli that put her so on edge? He had been perfectly correct and polite to her whenever she had encountered him—even the misunderstandings over their first meeting had been cleared up, so it couldn't be that. Was it simply because of the apparent effect he seemed to be having on the other members of staff?

Surely not, she told herself, it couldn't be because of that—and, besides, he couldn't help being handsome and attractive. So what was it? What elusive element was making her so wary of him? Usually Nadine prided herself on being a good judge of character, so was there some flaw about this man which she had subconsciously discovered? Was it that that was bugging her?

'Nadine!'

She jumped as someone tapped on her car window, startling her out of her daydream. Looking up, she found Seymour Russell peering into the car. She wound down the window. 'Hello, Seymour,' she said. 'You made me jump.'

'I thought you'd gone to sleep,' he said. 'You were miles away. I've been trying to attract your attention. I was afraid you were going to drive off without seeing me.'

'Sorry,' she said, 'I've got a few things on my mind.'

'Paul. . .?'

'No, no,' she said hastily, not wanting to get into a discussion as to what she had been thinking about. 'No, Paul's fine. What did you want to see me about, Seymour?'

'Only to remind you of our trip to the theatre at the weekend.'

'Did you think I might have forgotten?' She smiled.

'Well, I wasn't sure,' he replied, 'and I don't seem to have seen much of you in the last couple of days.'

'You saw me on the ward,' she said mischievously, knowing what his reaction would be.

'Yes, yes, I know. But I don't like to discuss private arrangements in front of the staff—you know that, Nadine,' he replied tetchily.

'I know, Seymour.' She smiled again. 'And I hadn't forgotten our date. How could I? I'm looking forward to this play as much as you are.'

'Good. Well, if I don't get another chance to see you before then, I'll pick you up around seven? All right?'

'Yes, of course.' She watched him affectionately as, with a wave of his hand, he crossed the car park to his own car—a beautifully restored vintage Wolseley. Seymour was a widower and Nadine knew that since the death of his wife, Kathleen, a few years previously he had been a very lonely man.

Through working together, they had discovered a mutual love of the theatre and their outings had become something of a regular occurrence. The arrangement suited her; it was pleasant to have a distinguished and handsome escort on occasion, and Seymour was both. The fact that he was at least twenty years her senior bothered neither of them, probably because neither of them had looked to take the relationship any further.

When Nadine reached Montague House, inserted her key in the lock and pushed open the door an appetising savoury smell wafted out to greet her.

'Something smells good,' she said as Fee appeared in the kitchen doorway.

'Spaghetti Bolognese,' replied Fee.

'I wonder why?' said Nadine in a resigned voice.

'He phoned to say he was moving in tonight, and I wanted to make him feel welcome,' said Fee defensively.

'I hope you haven't included his meals in the price of the room,' said Nadine severely.

'Of course not.' Fee looked suitably shocked. 'Besides, he said he would be eating out most of the time. I just thought tonight. . .'

'I know, you thought pasta would make him feel at home. You'll be telling me next you've opened another bottle of Chianti.'

'Funny you should say that, darling. . .'

'I give up!' Nadine rolled her eyes, then ran up the stairs to her own flat.

She found Paul, surrounded by school books, sprawled on the sofa in front of the television. A Coke can stood by his side and an empty crisp packet was on the arm of the sofa.

'Hi, Mum!' he called over his shoulder.

'Hello, love. Good day?'

'Pretty average, really.'

'What are you watching?' Nadine stared curiously at the screen, which seemed to be showing a particularly lurid sort of fantasy. 'Surely it's a bit early for that sort of thing?'

'It's a video. Scotty lent it to me. It's called *Revenge of the Barbarians*.'

'Any good?' she called as she headed for their tiny kitchen and dumped her bag.

'No, dead boring, actually.' Paul yawned and stood up. 'I only had it on while I was doing my maths homework.'

'I don't know how you can concentrate with all that noise,' said Nadine, slipping off her coat.

'I can't concentrate without it.' Paul grinned. 'We're having supper with Gran tonight, did you know?'

'Well, I rather gathered that was the idea.' Nadine sighed.

'Don't you want to?' asked Paul curiously. 'It's spaghetti Bolognese—my favourite.'

'Yes, I know, and of course I want to; it's very kind of Gran to cook for us. . .' she trailed off.

'But?' said Paul.

'What do you mean, "but"?' Nadine frowned.

'It sounded as if there was a "but" coming then,' said Paul knowingly. 'You said it was very kind of Gran to cook for us, then you stopped and it sounded as if a "but" should have come next.'

Nadine shrugged, not wanting to be drawn.

Paul seemed to have other ideas, for he followed her into her bedroom and watched while she pulled a loose cotton jumper over her shirt. 'It's because of him, isn't it?' he said at last.

Nadine sat down in front of her dressing-table and pulled her hair loose from the slide that secured it at the nape of her neck. 'Him?' she said, shaking her head, her smooth ash-blonde hair falling into the long straight bob she wore when not at work.

'Yes, Angelo.'

'Don't you mean Dr Fabrielli?' Her eyes met Paul's in the mirror.

'He said I was to call him Angelo,' said Paul.

Nadine drew in her breath sharply.

'You don't like him, do you, Mum?' said Paul curiously.

'I hardly know him. . .' Nadine shrugged and, picking up her hairbrush, began to brush her hair with long, sweeping strokes.

'It's not just because of the motorbike thing, is it?' Paul asked after a moment. 'I know how you hate motorbikes. . .'

'Of course not,' Nadine began, but Paul cut her short.

'So there is something? You don't like him?'

'I'm really not sure about him one way or the other, Paul,' she said, placing her hairbrush back on the dressing-table and standing up. 'He seems to have erupted onto the scene and taken over, and it's not only at work—he's to be here at my home as well. As if all that isn't enough, it seems I even have to have my supper with him into the bargain.'

Paul stared at her in apparent surprise. 'He's really nice, Mum,' he said at last. 'I'm sure you'll like him when you get to know him.'

'Yes, well, I hope I do, for all our sakes.' Nadine pulled a face.

'He likes you,' said Paul.

'He doesn't know me,' said Nadine abruptly, 'so he's hardly in a position to judge whether he likes me yet or not.'

'Well, he said he did,' said Paul, turning to the door.

Nadine had been about to hang some clothes in her wardrobe but she paused and looked at her son across the bed. 'What did he say?' she said, her curiosity suddenly getting the better of her.

Paul looked embarrassed, almost as if he was wishing that he hadn't started this particular conversation. 'It's a bit soppy, really,' he muttered.

'What is?' demanded Nadine.

'What he said about you.'

She stared at him. 'Well, come on,' she said when he remained silent, 'you can't leave it there—you've got to tell me now!'

'He said you were a lovely lady,' mumbled Paul. He would have bolted from the bedroom then, but Nadine called him back.

'When did he say that, Paul?' she demanded.

'Last night,' Paul replied, 'when we got back here on the bike. He said he couldn't believe you were my mum; that you didn't look old enough, and that he thought you were a lovely lady. Now, can I go? I want to ring Scotty and tell him his video was cra—sorry, rubbish.' He grinned then, Julian's grin, and disappeared out of the room.

Nadine stood rooted to the spot. Angelo Fabrielli had said that? That she was a lovely lady? It was nice to receive a compliment, she had to admit; she didn't get that many these days. . .

She pulled herself up sharply. What in the world was she thinking of? Compliments from Angelo Fabrielli were two a penny. From what she had heard from her colleagues, he admired and complimented every female he saw. Briskly she turned back to the wardrobe, and carried on tidying her clothes.

Later she heard Angelo arrive, the sound of the Harley Davidson on the drive, voices below in the hall and, when she looked out of her flat, from the landing she saw him carrying his bags to the bedsit on the first floor. As if he sensed her there on the landing above he glanced up and, when he saw her, he paused.

'Nadine.' He smiled. 'Hello.'

She nodded in response and was about to go back into her flat—to beat a hasty retreat—when Fee called up the stairs from the hall. 'Nadine, please could you show Angelo into his room? I can't leave the supper for the moment.'

She couldn't see why Angelo couldn't show himself in, but knew that it would appear rude to say so. With a sigh she went down the stairs, aware that he watched every step she took, and joined him on the first-floor landing. He was wearing his black leather gear, his dark hair was tousled from wearing his helmet and he carried a large holdall in each hand.

'Is this all you have?' she said.

'Paul is bringing up the rest but, yes,' he replied when she looked surprised, 'I travel light. I am in this country for such a short time that it seems foolish to accumulate too much baggage.'

'Oh yes, yes, of course,' she agreed. For the moment Nadine had forgotten that he was only on a temporary contract. 'Here's your room,' she said, pushing open the door and preceding him into the room.

'It is a nice room,' he said, looking round. 'Your mother showed it to me last night. I will be happy here.'

It was a nice room, Nadine thought, probably one of the best in the house. Facing south, it caught the after-noon sun and, with its magnolia walls, saffron-coloured furnishings and large bay window, it felt light and airy. 'You have your own shower through there.' Nadine nodded towards the far end of the room that was partitioned off.

'Yes,' Angelo nodded, 'and if I want a bath your mother says I am to use the bathroom on this landing.'

'Yes, but we also have to use that bathroom. . .' Nadine began.

'I will try not to inconvenience you,' he replied swiftly and, before she could say more, he went on, 'Your mother has also very kindly invited me to supper tonight. I have told her that usually I shall eat out, probably at the hospital. . .'

'Here's the rest of your gear.' Paul suddenly appeared

with another bag, Angelo's crash helmet and a squash racket. 'You like squash?' he added as he dumped the items on the bed.

'Yes,' said Angelo, 'do you?'

Paul nodded. 'I'll give you a game some time,' he said. 'Mum likes it as well, don't you, Mum? She's good, too—for a woman.'

'Is she?' Angelo turned and met Nadine's gaze. 'Maybe she also will give me a game some time?'

Nadine inclined her head then, prompted by some inner curiosity, she said, 'How did your game go tonight? Did you win?'

'Yes, I win,' he smiled.

'Karen will want a return game,' she said.

'Yes,' Angelo laughed. 'She was disappointed she did not win, but I buy her a drink afterwards to make up for it.'

We'll never hear the last of it tomorrow, Nadine thought. A game, a drink and the prospect of a return game. Idly she wondered where he had taken Lee Bevan—whether that date too had taken place at the sports centre or whether his plans for Lee had been of a more intimate nature. She dismissed the thought almost as quickly as it entered her head. It really was no concern of hers how Angelo Fabrielli conducted his private life.

To Nadine's annoyance, she found herself changing for dinner. She wasn't sure why she did—she only knew that she tried on several garments, studying herself critically in the full-length swivel mirror in her bedroom before finally settling on a long, stone-coloured, ribbed skirt with a matching long-line waistcoat and a crisp white blouse. She had decided to leave her hair loose but at the last minute changed her mind and tied it back, securing it at the nape of her neck with a black velvet bow.

At last she was ready and, telling herself that she would be glad when the evening was over, she took a deep breath, left the flat and went down the stairs.

The others were already in the kitchen and they looked up as she came into the room. Fee, Nadine noticed, had also changed and looked pretty and feminine in an Indian cotton skirt and an embroidered blouse, while Paul was in his habitual out-of-school wear of T-shirt and jeans. Angelo had changed from his black leathers and was wearing expensive-looking denims with a white, open-necked shirt and a tan suede waistcoat, which only succeeded in accentuating his tan and his dark Latin looks.

Nadine felt his gaze sweep over her as she stood in the doorway and suddenly, irrationally, she was glad that she had taken trouble over her appearance.

Fee's spaghetti Bolognese was excellent and Angelo made them all laugh by saying that because it had been Fee's intention to welcome him he had been expecting fish and chips or roast beef and Yorkshire pudding. They ate in Fee's kitchen around the old pine table which had been there for as long as Nadine could remember. Angelo seemed perfectly at home and Nadine could not help but think that it wasn't only because of the spaghetti and the Chianti.

He had an easy-going, laid-back way with him which implied that he could adapt and fit in with any situation. He talked to Paul about his hobbies, sport and his school, eventually bringing the subject round to his choice of career.

'Have you decided yet?' he asked. They had finished their meal and Fee was pouring delicious-smelling filter coffee from a cafetière.

'Oh, yes,' said Paul. 'I've always known. I want to be a doctor.'

'Foolish man.' Angelo laughed. 'Can he not be persuaded otherwise?' His eyes met Nadine's across the table.

'I suppose you could try,' said Nadine, 'but I don't think you'd get very far; there's never been any doubt in Paul's mind—at least not that I'm aware of.' She glanced at Paul, who laughed and shook his head.

'Mum's right,' he said. 'I have always wanted to be a doctor.' He paused. 'My father is a doctor,' he added.

In the silence that followed Angelo glanced from Nadine to Fee and then back to Nadine again, and with a shrug he began stirring his coffee. 'Just as long as you know what you are taking on,' he said to Paul. 'The long hours, the. . .the. . .' he searched for the right word '. . .the exhaustion,' he said at last. 'Yes, that is it—the exhaustion. . .'

'Sounds as if the conditions in your hospitals aren't a lot different from ours,' observed Nadine drily.

'Everyone always goes on about the long hours and the hard work,' said Paul suddenly and they all looked at him, 'but there must be a good side as well, otherwise no one would ever do it.'

'It's well paid, I believe, these days,' said Fee sipping her coffee.

'There are many better paid jobs,' said Angelo quietly. 'No, it is not the money, it is more. . .much, much more than that.' A passionate note had crept into his voice, and Nadine—watching him—found herself recalling the moment she had found him talking quietly to old Cyril Norman and then again when he had gone to reassure Josh Barnes before his trip to Theatre, cheering him up with his talk of motorbikes.

'Was it always your ambition to be a doctor?' asked Paul, turning his head to look curiously at Angelo who was sitting beside him.

'No, far from it.' Angelo laughed. 'I went through many career ideas before I found what I wanted.'

'But when you found it. . . Now do you have any regrets?' asked Paul eagerly.

Angelo shook his head. 'No,' he said, 'none at all. I feel as if I am doing what I was born to do.'

'I think that's wonderful' Fee clasped her hands together, then said, 'Tell us, Angelo, how did you come to be working in this country?'

'How I come to be in your country? Ah, I tell you. The surgeon I am working with in Italy,' he said, 'Giovanni Ligorio, he is an old colleague of your own Seymour Russell—Giovanni admires Seymour's techniques tremendously and wants me to work with him for a while to gain experience, you understand?' He glanced round the table and, when they nodded, he went on, 'So a visit is arranged for me.'

'I see,' Fee replied then, before anyone could say anything, she went on, 'Where exactly is your home, Angelo?'

'My family home is on the outskirts of Rome,' Angelo replied, 'but I have an apartment near the hospital which is in the heart of the city.'

'Do you spend a lot of time with your family?' Suddenly Nadine was curious, especially in view of the fact that Angelo had apparently chosen to live with a family while he was in England as opposed to living alone.

'I go home whenever I can;' he replied, 'whenever I am off duty.'

'You come from a large family?' asked Fee, pouring more coffee into Angelo's cup.

He nodded. 'I have two sisters and one brother. Both sisters are married and have children. My grandmother lives with my parents, and also my aunt—my father's sister.'

'That sounds wonderful,' said Fee with a sigh. 'That sort of lifestyle doesn't seem to work in this country any more.'

'Ah, that is because people have come not to expect it,' replied Angelo. 'Although,' glancing round the table at the three of them, he added, 'you seem to have made it work. In my country the family is everything—it comes first; it does not seem to occur to anyone there is any other option.

'Why, at weekends,' he grew more enthusiastic, gesticulating with his hands as he spoke, 'we all congregate at my parents' home. Sometimes as many as thirty sit down to a meal. . .and this meal, it will last for hours. Not only is there food and wine, there is talk—much, much talk—and everyone tells their news. . . Sometimes there is music. . .'

'Like I say, it sounds wonderful,' said Fee. 'All those generations getting along together.'

'Oh, we have arguments.' Angelo laughed. 'All the time, we argue but. . .' he shrugged '. . .we always seem to make up. . .' He paused and looked round the table— at Fee, who was still hanging on his every word, at Paul, who seemed fascinated by all he was hearing, and then at Nadine who, in spite of her reservations about this man coming to live in her home, had also found herself listening with interest to all he had to say about his home and his family.

'My grandmother is still the head of the family,' Angelo went on thoughtfully after a moment. 'Outwardly, of course, it is my father who controls the Fabrielli family and runs the family business, but everyone knows that if there is any problem it is his mother— my grandmother—who makes the final decision.'

'What is the family business?' asked Nadine.

'Jewellery,' replied Angelo briefly.

'Didn't your father want you to go into the business?' Suddenly Nadine was curious.

'Of course.' Angelo laughed. 'Again it was my grandmother who came to my rescue. When I told her I wanted to be a surgeon she said that was what I had to do. After that there was no further question.'

Paul stood up. 'In future, Gran,' he said, looking down at Fee, 'I'll just come to you if there's any question about my future. I won't bother asking Mum.'

'Just you try it,' said Nadine darkly.

Paul laughed. 'If I don't go and get on with some work there won't be any question about my future—I won't even get into the sixth form.'

Nadine, too, stood up as Paul disappeared from the

room. 'I'll wash up,' she said to Fee. 'You go and have a rest.'

'No, I'll help,' said Fee, beginning to stack the plates. 'You've been on your feet all day.'

'I will help, Nadine,' said Angelo, standing up.

'Oh, no, really, I can manage,' replied Nadine hastily.

'I insist,' he went on, picking up the large pot that had held the Bolognese and carrying it to the sink. 'That was an excellent meal, Fee; I enjoyed it very much; the least I can do is to help.'

'Oh, well, if you are sure,' said Fee, and with a help-less little shrug she left the kitchen, leaving Nadine alone with Angelo.

CHAPTER FIVE

THEY were silent at first, the silence a little unnerving after all the chatter and laughter of only moments before. While Nadine washed the dishes and stacked them in a plastic rack on the draining-board Angelo took one of Fee's red and white linen teatowels, and began drying them. It was such an ordinary, everyday task but Nadine felt uncomfortable, wishing she could hurry and so escape to her room.

'So, Paul—he wants to be a doctor,' said Angelo at last, breaking the silence that had grown between them to, it seemed, almost unmanageable proportions.

'Yes,' Nadine nodded, wondering what else she could add to a subject they had already discussed.

'His father,' said Angelo and Nadine stiffened, knowing now why the subject had been brought up again. 'Paul said he also is a doctor.'

Nadine nodded again, and when she offered no further information Angelo said, 'I say, "is," but should that perhaps have been "was"?—Forgive me, Paul's father is not dead?'

'No.' Nadine stared at the soap bubbles in the sink and shook her head. 'No, he isn't dead—at least, I presume he isn't. Let's put it this way—if he has died then no one saw fit to inform me. On the other hand, I doubt anyone would.' She was aware that Angelo had stopped wiping the plate in his hands and was staring at her.

'You are divorced?' he said quietly at last.

Nadine took a deep breath and, turning to face him, looked him squarely in the eye. 'I have never been married,' she said, 'so I can scarcely have been divorced.'

She saw his expression change, knew she had embarrassed him and secretly was glad. That would teach him not to pry into people's personal affairs—affairs they might not want to talk about or discuss, especially with a comparative stranger.

'I am sorry, Nadine.' His expression changed yet again, the dark eyes widening slightly—momentarily filled with remorse. 'I should not have asked. It was thoughtless. Please, forgive me.' All humour was gone now from those eyes that usually sparkled with amusement.

'It's all right.' Nadine gave a slight shrug and turned back to the water, feeling slightly guilty now of her haste to condemn him. 'It all happened a long time ago.'

If Angelo had asked more questions she would have dismissed them, and told him that she didn't wish to discuss the matter. As it was, he remained silent and, to her amazement, she found herself volunteering further details.

'We were both very young at the time,' she heard herself saying. 'I was doing my nursing training and Julian was a medical student. We had a brief, passionate affair and Paul was the result.'

'Did you love this man?' asked Angelo, his voice low.

Nadine hesitated before saying, 'I must have done at the time. . . Yes, yes, I did.'

'So why did he not marry you?'

Nadine shrugged. 'He couldn't handle it. Any of it—the fact that I was pregnant, the thought of his parents' anger when they found out, the threat to his career prospects.'

'So what happened?'

She was aware of Angelo's growing surprise, as if he was finding the whole thing hard to believe. But why he should react like that, she didn't know. She wasn't the first to have had that happen to her, and she very much doubted she would be the last. 'I told him to go,' she replied. 'To get out of my life and not come back. . .'

'And. . .?'

'He did just that. He went back to the north of the country, where his home was. Goodness knows what story he told them, but somehow he was able to continue his training there. I heard from him a couple of times. . . At first, he promised he would come back. . .when he qualified, he said. . .'

'And did he?'

'No.' Nadine shook her head, then stared out of the window into Fee's conservatory and the profusion of plants that filled the terracotta pots and tumbled from shelves. 'No,' she said at last, 'of course he didn't. Several years later I heard he'd married someone else— a GP's daughter, I think.'

'And you?' asked Angelo softly.

'Me?' she dragged her eyes from the plants and half turned her head in his direction.

'Yes, how did you feel when you heard he'd married someone else?'

'I don't think I cared by then,' she replied after a moment.

'So you didn't still love him?'

'Heavens, no.' Her head jerked up in surprise. 'I'd stopped loving him a long time before that.'

'But Paul? What about Paul?' Angelo leaned against the worktop and, folding his arms, watched her carefully.

'Well,' Nadine considered before she answered, 'Paul never knew Julian, of course, but I've always been at pains to preserve some sort of favourable image. . .' She frowned. 'I thought that was important, so we dwell more on the fact that Paul's father is a doctor than on the fact that he ran out on me.'

'That's generous of you.' Angelo raised one eyebrow, the gesture implying that he found it more than generous.

'Not really.' Nadine shrugged and, pulling the plug from the sink, released the soapy water. 'It was enough that Paul had to grow up without a father, without the added burden of thinking that his father was also a—'

she broke off, not finishing the sentence, as the water gurgled down the drain.

'Some women would have been bitter,' said Angelo, then thoughtfully he added, 'it could not have been easy for you, bringing up the boy alone.'

'No,' she admitted, 'it wasn't always easy, but my parents came to my rescue. They looked after Paul while I finished my training, then offered us the flat here in this house to live in. To be honest, I don't know what I would have done without them.'

'Your father. . .?'

She heard the question in Angelo's voice, and turned slightly. 'He died two years ago. . .' she said sharply then trailed off and, taking a deep breath, added, 'He was marvellous with Paul. . .'

'And you quite obviously miss him very much.'

She nodded, only too aware of the lump that had risen in her throat—the lump that was always there at any mention of her father. 'We all do,' she managed to say at last. 'My mother pretends she has got over his death but, at times, I wonder. Oh, she keeps busy, but even with us around I know she is still lonely. I don't suppose anything ever replaces a lifetime partner.'

Suddenly, in the silence that followed, Nadine realised how deep the conversation was becoming, and with a determined effort she straightened her shoulders. 'That's quite enough about me,' she said, her voice shaking slightly. 'What about you, Dr Fabrielli?'

'I think you hear enough about me during supper,' Angelo laughed and as she moved away from the sink he followed her, picking up the pile of plates he had dried and handing them to her one at a time as she placed them on the shelves of the kitchen dresser.

'About your home and family certainly,' she replied, 'and your career, of course, but nothing really about you.'

'What do you want to know?' He shrugged and laughed and she could not help but think how handsome he was, especially when he laughed and the whiteness of his teeth was in such contrast to his tanned skin and dark eyes.

'We've been talking about personal relationships— lifetime partners. You now know all about me, so maybe it's your turn to tell me about your private life.'

'Well, I am not married,' he said.

'I'm relieved to hear it,' she said and when she saw his look of amused amazement she hastily added, 'after the way you've been chatting up my nurses.'

'How do you mean?' He looked mystified. 'This chatting up—what is it, I don't understand. . .?'

'Oh. I think you do, Angelo,' she said, shaking her head. 'I think you know only too well what I mean.'

He was laughing by now. 'Well, maybe I do. But it is harmless: I just be friendly. I love women. . .I always love women. . . Why, in Italy, my friends and I. . .'

'Yes, yes, all right, I can imagine. . .' Nadine hastily cut him short. 'But please, go easy, won't you? Don't go breaking too many hearts while you are here. . . OK?'

'OK. . .' He smiled again, then said ruefully 'But my mother keeps telling me I must settle down, marry, have a family. . .'

'I doubt she meant to an English girl.'

'Maybe.' Angelo shrugged, then spread his hands. 'On the other hand, maybe not. . .' They both laughed.

'From what you've told me of your family I would say it would be expected that you marry a suitable girl from an Italian family.'

Angelo's eyes narrowed. 'Like I say, maybe that is what is expected, but, in the end, I will marry whom I wish.' His expression changed slightly as he spoke, and Nadine was aware of some emotion in the dark eyes that she hadn't seen before. It was fleeting, affording only a glimpse, but at the same time giving an insight to a side of this man's personality she hadn't yet seen. A side far removed from the easy-going charmer he had chosen so far to reveal. A side that hinted at a passionate determination to get what he wanted. Nadine suddenly felt that there was far more to the new registrar than she had at first thought.

Angelo went to his room shortly after that and Nadine went up to the flat but she found, to her surprise, that the irritation she had felt towards him previously seemed to have shifted. In fact, she felt quite light-hearted as she climbed the stairs, and was even humming to herself as she opened the door.

She was greeted by the sound of rock music and found Paul, lying full length on his stomach on the floor, an open book propped up only inches away from his nose.

She sighed but refrained from commenting. After a few minutes Paul turned the volume down until it was barely audible and grinned at her.

'Better?' he said.

'Much better,' she agreed and sank down onto the sofa, tucking her legs up beneath her and watching her son as he returned to his book.

'He's great, isn't he?' Paul said after a moment.

'Who?' Nadine knew who he meant but didn't want him to know that she too was thinking about their new lodger.

'Angelo, of course,' said Paul. 'Who do you think I meant?' When Nadine shrugged, he carried on. 'Well, I think he's great anyway.'

'Him or his motorbike?' Nadine raised her eyebrows but the irony was wasted on Paul.

'Both,' he replied simply. He was silent for a while and Nadine could have been forgiven for thinking he was reading again, but after a long pause he said, 'All that stuff about Rome and his family—it was really interesting. Normally I would have been bored with someone going on about all that, but he made it sound— I don't know—sort of exciting somehow, I suppose... didn't he?' He glanced over his shoulder at Nadine. 'Didn't he, Mum?' he repeated.

'Yes, yes,' she nodded. 'I guess he did. It certainly

sounds as if he comes from a fascinating background.'

'You've always wanted to go to Rome, haven't you?'

'Yes,' Nadine admitted. 'Yes, I have...but don't go telling Angelo that.'

'Why?' Paul grinned. 'Maybe he would invite you for a visit when he goes back.'

'That's what I would be afraid of,' replied Nadine drily.

'It would be brilliant, Mum... It really sounded dead good... And do you know what I think?' He turned his head to look at her.

'No, Paul,' she said, 'but I think you might be about to tell me.'

'I think Angelo fancies you.'

'Don't be ridiculous, Paul,' she said, and it came out a little more sharply than she had intended.

'What's ridiculous about it?' Paul sounded genuinely surprised.

'It just is, that's all.'

'But why?' Paul persisted. 'Why should it be?'

'For a start, he's far too young,' retorted Nadine.

'Is he?' Paul frowned. 'I wouldn't have thought so...'

'Well, he is... And, quite apart from that, he simply isn't my type so you can forget any notions like that,' she said firmly.

'Maybe.' Paul shrugged, 'but it doesn't alter the fact that he fancies you.'

She found herself thinking about what Paul had said later that night when she lay in bed. Usually she fell straight asleep almost as soon as her head touched the pillow but that night, for some reason, sleep eluded her and she found herself going over the events of the evening.

It had been quite ridiculous, of course, what Paul had said about Angelo fancying her—quite ridiculous.

But what had prompted her son to say such a thing?

Usually Paul would be the last person to make such an observation.

Maybe he had simply seen the way Angelo behaved, without realising that was the way he behaved towards any member of the opposite sex.

Yes, that was it. That had to be it.

Nadine turned onto her side in an attempt to find a more comfortable position.

If Paul had seen Angelo on the ward with the other nurses, she found herself reasoning a moment later, he would have realised that.

But supposing. . .just supposing Angelo was interested in her? What then?

But he wouldn't be, she thought. He was far too young for her.

And if that didn't matter to him? What then? How would she feel? How would she react?

The idea was preposterous. Nadine burrowed further into her pillow.

But just supposing he was to ask her out? Would she go?

Abruptly she turned onto her back again and stared up at the ceiling. If he did, and if she were to go, how on earth would she explain it to the others at work? She could just picture it—Jayne's amusement, Karen's anger, Lee's anguish and Ruth. . .well, what on earth would Ruth's reaction be? She shuddered at the thought. No, the very idea was as she had at first thought—completely ludicrous.

What had been rather nice, though, was the fact that her teenage son should have even thought that the young Italian doctor might be interested in her.

It was with that oddly comforting thought uppermost in her mind that Nadine finally fell asleep.

The following day all such fanciful thoughts had long flown in the early morning flurry to get to work and to make sure that Paul got up in time for school. By the time Nadine finally dashed from the house it was to find that there was no sign of Angelo Fabrielli or his Harley Davidson.

As she started her car engine she realised she was relieved he had already gone; that she had in some way been dreading that he would suggest they shared transport and travel to work together. It would make sense, she knew, but she also knew, and quite unreasonably so, that she didn't want him beside her in the car in the early mornings—the time she spent getting her act together for the day ahead—any more than she wanted, or could imagine, for that matter, herself perched on the back of that black monster of a motorbike of his.

She soon forgot Angelo when the demands of her job took over. One of the first tasks of the day was to admit a member of the hospital's own staff for a laminectomy operation.

Jennifer Dickinson was a senior staff nurse on one of the hospital's medical wards. Her job had involved many years of nursing long-term chronically sick patients, especially the elderly. Her present painful and disabling back condition had arisen from the vast amount of heavy lifting that her job had entailed, resulting in a severely misplaced disc. Jennifer had initially been very reluctant to resort to surgery, and had only done so after exploring every other alternative.

These alternatives, Nadine knew, had included oesteopathy, lengthy sessions with a chiropractor, physiotherapy and, more recently, acupuncture.

'I really thought the acupuncture was going to do the trick,' Jennifer confided as Nadine filled in the admission forms, 'but I was wrong. Things were fine for a while but then the pain was back, more crippling than ever. When I saw Seymour Russell he said he thought the time had finally come for surgery.'

'Did Seymour know about all the other alternatives?'

asked Nadine, glancing through Jennifer's medical records.

'Oh, yes,' Jennifer replied. 'He didn't seem to mind. In fact, he even encouraged me to try the acupuncture.'

'Seymour's very good like that,' agreed Nadine. 'Some surgeons have no patience with alternatives— they think surgery is the only answer, but I think Seymour sees it as the last resort when all else has failed. Now, tell me, Jennifer, what painkillers have you been taking?'

'You name it, I've had it.' Jennifer pulled a face and shifted in her chair to try and find a more comfortable position.

'Let's put it this way—' Nadine gave a sympathetic smile '—what are you taking at the moment?'

'Dihydrocodeine.'

'Right.' Watched by Jennifer, Nadine wrote the name of the drug in the appropriate space on the admission form.

'Are you still going out with Seymour?' asked Jennifer after a moment.

'We go out occasionally.' Nadine looked up.

'Nothing serious, then?'

'No.' She shook her head. 'Nothing serious—just good friends, as they say. I expect Seymour will be up to see you later; I understand he has agreed to do your op?'

'Yes,' Jennifer nodded. 'I gather it was his day off and it should apparently have been his senior reg, Tom Selby, but Seymour told me he would do it himself.'

'Seymour's like that. . .' said Nadine then, standing up, she said, 'Well, I think that's all for the moment, Jen, so if you'd like to go and get yourself sorted out? Second bay, ladies section, third bed on the right. It's a nice bed, good view. . .'

'It had better be,' muttered Jennifer, wincing with pain as she attempted to stand up.

'Come on, I'll give you a hand.' Picking up her holdall

in one hand, Nadine slipped her other hand under Jennifer's elbow and assisted her out of the office and onto the ward.

The bed which had been allocated to Jennifer was next to Peggy Simpkins and as they approached Peggy, who was sitting in an upright chair beside the bed with her leg resting on a footstool, looked up with interest from the magazine she was reading.

'Hello, love,' she said to Jennifer.

Jennifer's reply was barely audible, uttered as it was through pain-gritted teeth.

'In pain, are you?' Peggy's homely face took on an expression of sympathy. 'I know just how you feel. I was the same when I came in. You ask Sister there. Wasn't I, Sister? Wasn't I just like that? Hardly move, I couldn't. You want to see me now. Fairly race down that corridor I do. They'll put you right, love. Just you wait and see.'

'I hope you're right,' muttered Jennifer as Nadine gently helped to lower her onto the chair beside her bed.

'Oh, they will,' Peggy went on relentlessly. 'Marvellous they are in here. Even the food's good. I wasn't too sure at first. You hear stories, don't you? But I speak as I find and, I must say, I don't have no complaints. Oh, here comes my doctor now. Comes in every morning to see me, he does. Hello, Doctor.'

'*Buon giorno*, Peggy.'

Nadine looked up quickly.

'I love it when he says that,' said Peggy. 'He sounds just like Al Pacino. . .'

'How are you this morning?' As he spoke Angelo glanced at Nadine and then at Jennifer, who had paused midway to the chair and was gaping at him, then he smiled down at Peggy.

While Peggy proceeded to tell him exactly how she was Nadine whisked the curtains around Jennifer's bed, enclosing them both inside. As Jennifer finally collapsed onto the chair with a deep sigh of relief, she looked up at Nadine.

'Who is *that*?' she mouthed, jerking her thumb towards Angelo on the other side of the curtain.

'Seymour's temporary reg,' Nadine mouthed back.

'Wow!' gasped Jennifer helplessly and Nadine, now well used to feminine reaction to Angelo, doubted that Jennifer's sudden weakness came solely from her condition.

After helping Jennifer unpack her bag and get undressed, Nadine persuaded her to lie flat on the bed. 'You'll be much more comfortable than sitting,' she said. 'I'm sure Seymour will be along to see you soon.'

'If not, he can send his registrar,' murmured Jennifer. 'I may be flat on my back but I can still recognise a fine specimen of manhood when I see one.'

Nadine was smiling when she stepped from between the curtains and found Angelo still talking to Peggy. Drawing the curtains so that Jennifer could see what was going on in the ward, she was about to ask Angelo if he was due to assist in Theatre that day when Lee Bevan suddenly appeared.

'Nadine,' she said, carefully avoiding Angelo's eye, 'A and E have just phoned. They have an emergency for us.'

'Are they still on the phone?' asked Nadine.

'Yes. The casualty officer wants a word.'

With a last reassuring nod to Jennifer, Nadine made her way past Angelo and Peggy and down the ward to her office where she picked up the telephone receiver from where it was lying on the desk.

'Sister Hadley,' she said.

'Hello, Sister. Ali Turiq here. Do you have a bed, please?'

'What is it, Dr Turiq?' Nadine asked.

'We have a man who has fallen from scaffolding. His X-rays show a fractured femur and multiple fractures to his pelvis. Dr Selby will be operating later this morning.'

'Very well,' replied Nadine, 'have him sent up.' As she replaced the receiver she suddenly had the feeling that she was not alone—that someone had followed her into the office. Without turning, she knew that it was Angelo. She wasn't sure how she knew—she just did. His presence in the room was like some tangible thing.

'I shall be assisting with Mrs Dickinson's laminectomy this morning,' he said, not waiting for her to turn, as if he too knew that she was aware of his presence.

When she at last turned to face him Nadine suddenly remembered Paul's words of the previous evening, and of how he reckoned Angelo Fabrielli fancied her. The thought, coming as it did at that moment of intense awareness and just as her eyes met his, was disconcerting to say the least and, to her dismay, Nadine felt her cheeks redden. She knew immediately that Angelo had seen her embarrassment; could tell by the questioning look that came into his eyes.

'Is there something wrong, Sister Hadley?' he asked softly. He used the form of address that she had requested on the ward even though there was no one else in earshot, but his tone—as gentle as a caress—only added to Nadine's discomfort.

'No,' she said quickly, too quickly, 'there's nothing wrong, Dr Fabrielli. Why should there be?'

'No reason,' he shrugged. 'It's just that you seem. . .' His eyes roamed over her face, her hair tucked beneath her cap and her face again, coming at last to rest on her mouth. 'I don't know. . .' His voice was so soft now that it was almost a whisper. 'I can't find the words. . . my English. . .it fails me sometimes. . .'

'Maybe that's just as well,' replied Nadine shakily. How dared he make her feel that way. . .and with just a look, as well? In a desperate attempt to pull herself together, she said, 'Maybe you would like to have a word with Mrs Dickinson, if you are assisting Mr Russell.'

'You think I should?' he asked, and his voice was normal now.

'I'm sure she would appreciate it,' Nadine was recovering rapidly. 'Mr Russell will be along to see her soon, but a little extra reassurance wouldn't go amiss.'

'OK. I go, then.' He seemed to linger as if he wanted to say more but Nadine gave him no chance, switching on her computer and busying herself with disks.

When he finally left her office she breathed a huge sigh of relief. She couldn't imagine what had possessed her to behave in such a foolish manner. Why, for one moment there she had felt like a teenager about to embark on her first date. Not only had she blushed—something she hadn't been aware of doing for years—but her knees had grown quite weak and her mouth had gone dry. And as if all that wasn't enough, now—even now after he'd gone—her heart was thumping in a most uncomfortable way.

And really, she told herself firmly, this was all quite ridiculous. There was no way the young registrar could be remotely interested in her, and she certainly wasn't interested in him.

At last, when she had given herself time to recover, she opened her office door and peered out onto the ward. Mercifully there was no sign of Angelo. No doubt by now he had gone down to Theatre to scrub up. Glancing past the nurses' station to the men's section of the ward, Nadine saw that Jayne was receiving the patient from A and E who had just been brought up in the lift.

Intending to go and assist her staff nurse, Nadine left the office but as she hurried past the half-open door of the sluice she heard a snuffling sound coming from inside. She stopped and, something prompting her to investigate, she pushed open the sluice door and looked inside to find Lee Bevan, standing at the sink.

When the girl turned Nadine saw that her eyes were red and watering.

'What is it, Lee?' she asked, but at the same time she

had the feeling that she knew only too well what was
wrong. 'You'd better tell me what this is all about,' she
added, her heart sinking.

CHAPTER SIX

'IT's that bitch, Karen Ashton,' sniffed Lee.

'So, just what is Karen supposed to have done?' asked Nadine, knowing full well what she was about to hear.

'She's after Angelo.' Lee blew her nose in an already soggy tissue.

'Angelo?' Nadine raised her eyebrows, playing for time and wondering how she should handle this.

'Yes,' gulped Lee, 'Dr Fabrielli. Like a fool, I told Karen that he asked me out last week. Now I hear she went out with him last night! She must have thrown herself at him. You know what she's like. . . She always—'

'Wait a minute, Lee,' Nadine interrupted. 'Let's take this slowly, shall we? First, I suggest we find somewhere a little more discreet—like my office. Come on.'

Lee followed Nadine out of the sluice and into her office, where Nadine indicated for her to take a seat before she too sat down behind her desk. She was suddenly afraid that if she didn't sit down her legs would be in danger of giving way.

'Right, now, Lee.' She took a deep breath. 'Tell me all about it. From the beginning, please.'

'Well,' Lee began after a moment's reflection, 'I suppose it really all goes back to when I was going out with Dean Gardiner—you know Dean, he's a paramedic?'

'Yes, I know Dean,' said Nadine with a frown, 'but I'm not sure what he has to do with any of this.'

'Well, it was Karen Ashton who split us up, you know,' said Lee. 'She's always been dead jealous of me, anyway; she didn't really want Dean. And now she's doing the same thing again. Just because Angelo showed interest in me she's jealous, and is trying to

muscle in.' She sniffed again, but at least she had
stopped crying.

'So, did Dr Fabrielli give you any reason to think you
had something special together?' asked Nadine. Suddenly she was curious. Usually she was fairly indifferent
to the squabbles amongst the younger members of her
staff over their boyfriends but this seemed different, and
she found herself waiting for Lee's answer.

'I felt there was something from the moment we met,'
said Lee, 'and I'm certain he felt the same,' she added.

Nadine was about to ask the girl if she thought that
she was the only one to have been affected by the arrival
of the young Italian, but, fearing the question may be
misconstrued, she remained silent and instead forced
herself to try and concentrate.

'You can tell, can't you?' Lee appealed. 'When someone is really attracted to you it shows. It's right there
in their eyes—the way they look at you. . .isn't it,
Nadine?'

'What?' Nadine looked up, startled, to find that while
Lee had been talking about that certain look in a person's
eyes she herself had been inadvertently picturing Angelo
Fabrielli and the look that had been in his eyes only
moments earlier, when he had been looking at her.

'Oh yes, yes, absolutely,' she managed to reply at
last, at the same time wondering what on earth the girl
would think if she could read her thoughts and whether
or not the look in question was one the registrar gave
to all women, or one he reserved for a chosen few.

'Anyway,' Lee gulped, blissfully unaware of
Nadine's thoughts, 'it didn't take long for him to ask
me out.'

'How long exactly?' asked Nadine politely.

'Only a few days.'

'So, where did he take you?'

'Oh, it was only for a drink in the social club,' Lee
replied quickly, 'but I felt it was going to lead to more—
you know what I mean.' She gave a meaningful nod.

'I'm pretty certain he was going to ask me to go out for a meal with him.'

'What happened?' asked Nadine, curious again.

'What do you mean?' A dreamy, faraway expression had come into Lee's eyes.

'You said you thought he was about to ask you to go out for a meal with him.' Nadine struggled to hold onto her patience. 'So did he?'

'No, his bleeper went off,' said Lee then, when she caught sight of Nadine's incredulous expression, she said quickly. 'He was on call, I knew that. But. . .' she gave a deep sigh '. . .I also knew, from the conversation and from the way he was looking at me, that he was leading up to asking me to go out with him again. He even walked me to my car before he went back to the ward. . . Honestly, Nadine, he was so romantic. . . And when he kissed me. . .well!'

'He kissed you?' Nadine threw the girl a quick glance.

'Yes,' Lee sighed and Nadine had a sudden, quite unreasonable desire to shake her. After a moment the girl continued, 'Well, it wasn't a proper kiss, if you know what I mean, it was only a brush of his lips, but then he ran his fingers down my cheek and told me how much he admired blonde English girls with blue eyes. He said where he comes from most of the girls are very dark.

'Honestly, Nadine, I know he fancied me. . . Anyway, like a fool I didn't keep it to myself. I told Karen Ashton. . .and now this morning she comes in and tells me that she went out with Angelo last night! Do you know, I could kill her!'

'Calm down, Lee.' Nadine was startled by the vehemence in the girl's voice.

'I tell you, Nadine, I'm sick of her—first Dean and now Angelo. Honestly, I could. . .'

'Did Karen tell you where they went last night?' asked Nadine hurriedly when Lee's eyes began to gleam again with angry tears.

'Not really—' Lee shook her head '—but she more or less said she went back to his place afterwards... and we all know what that means!'

Nadine remained silent for a moment, considering, then, coming to a rapid decision, she said, 'If I were you, Lee, I would take a lot of what Karen says with a pinch of salt—'

'But supposing it's true?' Lee interrupted, 'Supposing she did go back with him? D'you know, I really could kill her. In fact, I think I probably will.' She flashed a furious glance towards the door.

'Lee,' said Nadine hastily, 'would you feel any better if I were to tell you that I know for a fact that Dr Fabrielli didn't take Karen back to his place last night?'

Lee had started to blow her nose again but she paused and stared at Nadine. 'How do you know that?' she asked in surprise.

'Let's just say that I do...' Nadine tried to sound matter-of-fact but she could see from Lee's expression that the girl didn't believe her. And why should she? After all, what would Nadine know about Angelo Fabrielli's movements outside of working hours unless...unless she herself were somehow involved with him...? Nadine threw the girl a sharp glance. There was no way she wanted her thinking that.

Why, at this rate it might only be a matter of time before rumours would be flying around the orthopaedic unit about the Italian doctor and herself, and that was the last thing Nadine wanted. She had already told Ruth about her lodger, but Ruth was a very close person and had obviously not chosen to divulge the information to anyone else.

'Lee...' Nadine took another deep breath '...I do happen to know a little more about Dr Fabrielli than you might realise.'

The girl stared at her with startled interest and Nadine went on quickly, 'You see, he is in lodgings at my home.'

'At your home. . .?' The girl's voice rose dis-
believingly.

'Well, it's my mother's house, really,' explained
Nadine hurriedly. 'My son and I have a flat there, and
my mother lets another of the rooms as a bedsit. It was
empty, and she offered it to Ange—to Dr Fabrielli. He
moved in last night and I happen to know he was on
his own. . .' she trailed off, then added, 'if that puts your
mind at rest.'

Lee stared at her and Nadine heard some inner little
voice telling her not to meddle in the love lives of her
staff. That, however, proved to be far from easy, having
gone so far, for slowly Lee said, 'Are you saying that
Karen was lying—that she never went back to Angelo's
place with him? That she never even went out with
him at all?'

'Hold on, Lee,' Nadine said hastily. 'I'm not exactly
saying that. All I am saying is that Angelo's place happens to be my place, and that Karen certainly wasn't
there with him last night. I'm not saying they didn't go
out at all. In fact, I believe they did, but much earlier
in the evening.'

'Do you know where they went?' demanded Lee

'That really isn't for me to say.' Nadine stood up.
'What I am trying to say, Lee, is that you shouldn't let
Karen wind you up—or anyone else for that matter—
and where Angelo Fabrielli is concerned my advice to
you is to go easy. He is a very attractive young man.
He is a guest in this country, and I have a feeling that
when he returns to Italy he is going to leave a trail of
broken hearts behind him. . . So just watch yourself,
Lee, and for goodness' sake, play it cool.'

'All right.' Lee nodded but she seemed calmer.
'Thanks, Nadine,' she mumbled, then she stood up. 'I'd
best get back to work,' she said.

'Yes, I think you had.' Nadine gave a tight little smile.
'Jayne will be tearing her hair out if she doesn't get
some help soon.'

She watched as the girl left her office then she sank down onto her chair again for a moment and sat, drumming her fingers on the desk and staring out of the window at the town of Hawksford that lay spread out before her.

She hoped that she'd handled the situation correctly. It was always difficult when two members of staff clashed over something, especially over a man, but in this case it was different because somehow she herself seemed involved. And that was crazy really because she wasn't, at least only insomuch that Angelo was lodging at her house. It wasn't as if he'd asked her out or anything like that.

With a sigh she stood up and glanced in the mirror. And let's face it, she ruefully told her reflection, there's not much chance of that happening—not while he is surrounded by so many attractive young nurses.

On the other hand, hadn't Lee just said that Angelo actually preferred blonde English girls? Thoughtfully Nadine tucked a strand of her own ash-blonde hair inside her cap. Ah, but he had surely meant young English girls, not matrons with teenage sons—even if the teenage son in question had suspected him of fancying his mother.

And hold on a moment, she scathingly told her reflection, she'd reasoned all this out before, and even if by some remote chance he did find her attractive, there was no way, not in a million years, that she would be interested in him.

When she returned to the ward Nadine found that the new patient was a middle-aged man called Bob Jenkins. He was a self-employed builder and had slipped from scaffolding at a house where he had been building an extension. He had been given strong analgesics in A and E to help control the severe pain he was suffering from his fractured femur and his pelvic injuries.

Jayne and Ruth had admitted him to the ward and were preparing him for Theatre, while Karen was trying to calm his distraught wife who had just arrived. At the same time the orthopaedic unit's physiotherapist, Hans van Orden, was trying to persuade a reluctant Cyril Norman to begin some gentle exercise.

Nadine checked that Lee seemed to have pulled herself together and was assisting Enid Farrow, another of their health support team, with Josh Barnes's bed bath. She was soon absorbed into the busy routine once more with countless demands on her time, and the personal problems of her staff—and indeed her own—were pushed to the back of her mind.

Bob Jenkins was the first to go to Theatre and was escorted down by Ruth to Theatre 1, where Tom Selby was waiting to attempt to repair the man's shattered body.

Before Ruth returned to the ward the porters, Dave and Ken, arrived to take Jennifer Dickinson down to Seymour Russell who, that morning, was operating in Theatre 2.

Nadine, glancing round to see who she could send as escort, found that everyone seemed to be fully occupied. 'Looks like you'll have to put up with me.' She grinned at Jennifer who, drowsy from her pre-med, was lying on the porters' trolley.

'It's no more than I would expect. . .nothing less than Ward Sister,' joked Jennifer.

After a brief word with Jayne, who automatically took control if she left the ward, Nadine joined Dave and Ken and accompanied them on the walk through the long corridors to the operating theatres.

As they neared their destination Ken looked down at Jennifer, whom he knew well from her work on the medical ward. 'You OK, Jen?' he asked.

'No,' said Jennifer. 'I think I've changed my mind. Is that allowed at this point, Sister?'

'Well, I wouldn't mind,' said Nadine, 'but I doubt Seymour would be too happy, especially when he could have been on the golf course this morning.'

'On second thoughts, maybe I'd better keep this particular date,' mumbled Jennifer, her speech becoming quite slurred from the effects of the drugs she'd had. 'Talking of dates,' she went on as they approached the theatre door, 'that gorgeous Italian said he would be around. . .'

They swept into the ante-theatre where Simon Farrington—the anaesthetist—the theatre sister and Angelo Fabrielli were all waiting.

'Speak of the devil,' said Nadine drily then, glancing at Angelo, she said, 'We were just talking about you, Dr Fabrielli.'

Dressed in his green theatre gown, the dark eyes sparkled over the top of his blue mask. 'Mrs Dickinson,' he murmured, 'you kept our date. I am honoured, enchanted. . .'

'Yuk!' said Dave, pulling a face.

'Oh, don't stop him,' said Jennifer, 'I like it.'

'Jennifer, my dear.' Seymour, similarly gowned and masked, strode into the ante-room from Theatre.

'I haven't had so much attention for years,' murmured Jennifer happily as the anaesthetist also moved towards her.

Nadine was about to go when Angelo caught her eye. 'I have been thinking,' he said, 'maybe you would allow me to cook supper tonight?'

'Oh, I don't think that's necessary, Dr Fabrielli,' she said quickly, at the same time out of the corner of her eye noticing that Seymour, who had been about to go back into the theatre, had stopped and was listening.

'No, really, I would like to,' Angelo said then, as Seymour turned and stared at him in surprise, he went on, 'and, besides, it's the least I can do, especially after last night.'

Nadine fled out of the ante-theatre—away from Seymour's astonished expression, away from Angelo's puzzled stare, the porters' knowing looks and away from the silly grin which had settled on Jennifer Dickinson's face in the seconds before she sank into oblivion.

'What in the world was he on about?' Seymour peered over his glasses at her. It was early afternoon and the consultant had just called into the ward to see Jennifer, before going home.

'What was who on about?' Nadine tried to sound innocent, but knew full well what he meant.

'Our young Italian friend,' said Seymour. 'Whatever was all that about it being the least he could do to cook supper?'

'Oh, that,' Nadine said, picking up Jennifer's folder from her desk. 'Well, I suppose he just thought he would return the compliment.'

'I don't understand.' Seymour frowned.

'Well, my mother cooked supper for us all last night, so I guess Dr Fabrielli thought he would do the same tonight.'

'I still don't quite see what your mother was doing cooking supper for Angelo Fabrielli in the first place.' Seymour looked more bewildered than ever.

Nadine took a deep breath and wondered just how many more times she would need to explain. First it had been to Ruth, then to Lee and now Seymour.

'I know he's lodging at your place,' said Seymour unexpectedly.

'Oh. You do?' She looked up quickly.

'Yes,' Seymour nodded, 'he mentioned it in Theatre. I just wondered why he should feel obliged to cook for you, that's all, or, come to that, why your mother felt she had to cook for him.'

'I don't think she felt she had to,' replied Nadine wearily. 'I think she just thought it would be a nice gesture, that's all. Would help to make Angelo feel welcome.'

'That was very charitable of her,' replied Seymour—rather pompously, Nadine thought—but before she

could say any more he went on, 'I must say I was
surprised when young Fabrielli said he had moved into
your house. I had arranged for him to stay in hospital
accommodation while he is in this country. I would have
thought that was quite adequate.'

'Adequate, maybe,' said Nadine, 'but rather soulless,
you have to admit that, Seymour. He told my mother
he preferred being with a family.'

'He should have told me that at the start. I would
have made other arrangements.' Seymour was beginning
to sound tetchy. 'Are you sure it isn't going to be an
imposition, Nadine, because if it is. . .?'

'Oh, no, Seymour,' she heard herself say, 'no, really.
It's fine and we were looking for another lodger
anyway.'

'Well, if you're certain. . . And I must say, he seems
a pleasant enough young fellow. Comes from a very
good family, I believe. According to my ex-colleague,
Giovanni Ligorio, the Fabrielli family is also very
wealthy.'

'So I believe,' replied Nadine. 'Sounds like a large
family, as well.'

'Yes. These old Italian families are quite old-
fashioned, you know—very into bloodlines and
inheritance and that sort of thing. Mind you, I should
imagine there's quite a bit to inherit there, and young
Angelo's the eldest—family business is jewellery, I
understand.'

'Perhaps we could keep that quiet,' said Nadine, a
note of desperation in her voice.

'How do you mean?' asked Seymour, raising his
eyebrows.

'I'm having enough trouble with my nurses drooling
over your registrar as it is, without them knowing he
stands to inherit a fortune as well.'

Seymour laughed.

'But I'm sure you didn't come here to discuss either
Dr Fabrielli's domestic arrangements or the romantic

inclinations of my nurses,' said Nadine briskly, 'so shall
we go and see how Jennifer Dickinson is recovering?'

True to his word, Angelo did cook supper for them
that night—a delicious Italian dish, which had them all
guessing as to the ingredients of the sauce. He also
provided the wine—an excellent bottle of Bardolino.

'This will have to stop,' protested Nadine, 'wine every
night. . .'

'In my country. . .' Angelo shrugged and refilled
her glass.

'I think it's a wonderful idea,' said Fee with a laugh.

'Don't you have a rehearsal tonight?' asked Nadine
severely.

'Yes, but not until later,' replied Fee airily.

'So, how do you think you're going to get there?'
asked Nadine. 'You certainly can't drive yourself, and
I've been drinking.'

Fee clapped her hand over her mouth. 'Oh!' she said.
'I forgot. I'm not used to this lifestyle. . .I shall have to
get a taxi!'

'It'll cost you, Gran,' said Paul seriously. 'It's miles
to the theatre.'

'It is not a problem,' said Angelo. 'I have had only
one glass of wine. That, I believe, is permitted?' He
glanced at Nadine, and when she nodded he went on,
'I will take you to your rehearsal, Fee.'

'You mean you will drive Gran's car?' asked Paul.

'No,' Angelo shook his head, 'I had not thought that.
I thought the bike.'

Nadine's head jerked up in surprise, Fee gave a little
shriek and Paul let out a great guffaw. 'Oh, brilliant,'
he said, 'Super-Gran!'

'There is a problem?' Angelo looked from Nadine to
Fee then back to Nadine again.

'Well,' said Nadine, 'I really don't think Mum should,
you know—'

'Why not?' demanded Fee, and everyone looked at her.

'You might have a giddy turn, Mum,' protested Nadine, 'and it's cold tonight,' she added helplessly.

'You're just envious,' said Fee. 'Besides, I would like a ride and if Angelo is prepared to take me, then I'm prepared to take a chance.'

Paul was still laughing after they'd finished their meal and he took himself off to Scotty's house.

Angelo told Fee to dress warmly, then, while Nadine cleared the supper dishes, he took her off to her rehearsal.

Nadine shuddered as she heard the Harley roar away up the road and with a sigh she took herself upstairs to her flat.

She carried out a few necessary household tasks and had just chosen a CD from her opera collection and sat down on the sofa when there came a knock on the flat door.

It came as no surprise to find Angelo standing on the landing, his crash helmet under his arm. 'Don't tell me,' said Nadine, 'you had an accident. . .'

'Of course not.' He looked so shocked that for one moment she almost wished she hadn't said it.

'Well, then. . .' she gave a light laugh '. . .at the very least my mother will have fallen off the back.'

'You have a very low opinion of motorbikes, haven't you?' he said.

'Yes,' she replied bluntly. 'I've seen too much of the damage they can do to young lives.'

'I told you before,' he said softly, 'it is not the bikes — it is the riders.'

'Maybe. . .' She shrugged. 'So, was my mother all right?'

'Of course,' he said, 'that is what I came to tell you. She enjoyed her ride.'

'Good, well, thank you for taking her.'

'Your mother. . .' he hesitated '. . .she said you were

envious. . .I think perhaps you, too, would like a ride?'

'No way!' Nadine held up her hands in mock horror.
'I think perhaps you don't like motorbikes because
you've never been on one.'

'That's got nothing to do with it,' she protested.

'So you have been on one?'

'As a matter of fact, no, I haven't,' she admitted
at last.

'Then how can you possibly know?' he said softly.
'But maybe. . .maybe it's the fear?'

'What do you mean?' Nadine looked indignantly
at him.

'Maybe it's that you are afraid.'

'Of course I'm not afraid,' she protested. She certainly
didn't want him thinking that, especially after her mother
had shown no fear.

'Prove it!' Angelo laughed again, his teeth white
against his tanned skin.

'What do you mean, prove it?' she demanded.

'What I say. If you aren't afraid, prove it by coming
for a spin with me.'

'What, now?' She was half indignant, half
incredulous.

'Why not now? Paul is out, Fee is out.'

'What's that got to do with it?'

'If you really are afraid and they were here, they
would find out. As it is. . .'

He was issuing her with a challenge, and she knew
it. 'Right,' she said abruptly, 'I'll get my coat.' She
could not help but see the delighted flicker of amusement
in his eyes.

'Make it a warm one,' he called from the landing as
she turned and stalked through the flat to her bedroom.
'And a scarf. You were quite right about one thing,
Nadine, it is cold tonight.'

CHAPTER SEVEN

IT WAS cold, with a hint of frost in the air.

Nadine wound the scarf round her neck and tucked the ends inside her jacket, before taking the crash helmet that Angelo handed to her. After she'd eased it on her head and fastened it there came a point, as she watched Angelo mount the machine, that she almost chickened out.

After all, what the hell did it matter if he had issued her with a challenge? She didn't have to take it up, for heaven's sake. And if he did think she was scared, did it really matter? Did it?

He nodded towards her and indicated for her to mount the pillion seat behind him.

Gritting her teeth, she stepped forward. It was like being inside another world, encased in the crash helmet—a world where sound was muted, vision restricted. Nadine wasn't sure she liked that and she hadn't even got onto the bike yet.

Cautiously she put one foot on the step and, placing her hands on Angelo's shoulders, steadied herself, before mounting the pillion.

Confronted with his leather-clad body, she sat well back on her seat—her hands folded primly in her lap.

'You will need to hold on,' he called over his shoulder.

'Oh, right,' she said, and uncertainly she gingerly put her hands either side of his waist.

He looked down. 'Don't you have gloves?' he called again.

'No.' She paused, feeling silly. 'Should I get some?'

'It doesn't matter. Put your hands up inside my jacket.'

'No,' she said hurriedly, 'no, thanks, I shall be all right.'

'Do as I say,' he said. He spoke sharply. It was the first time that Nadine had heard such authority in his voice and, after only a moment's hesitation, she found herself meekly obeying him and pushing her hands up under his jacket, where they came into contact with his sweatshirt—warm from the heat of his body.

'That is better,' he said. 'It will get even colder, your hands would be frozen in a very short time.'

It was pleasant, Nadine was forced to admit as her hands rapidly grew warm, but at that moment the bike moved, and every ounce of her concentration was taken in holding tightly onto Angelo and in staying astride the bike.

They drew out of Acacia Avenue onto the main road and down the hill and, by the time they reached Hawksford's main shopping thoroughfare and the brightly lit shop windows flashed past, Nadine felt her fear begin to seep away.

The motorbike somehow seemed much more solid and safe than she had ever thought it would, and the warmth of Angelo's body was reassuring.

When they left the shops behind and headed out of town towards the open road she had become quite accustomed to the balance and realised that she was even beginning to enjoy herself.

'Are you all right?' Angelo called once over his shoulder.

'Yes, fine,' she shouted back, but her words, she guessed, were whipped away by the wind, so, instead, when he half turned his head again she instinctively tightened her grip on his body.

The response seemed to satisfy him, and he appeared to settle himself deeper onto his seat.

When they reached the wide dual carriageway and Angelo accelerated the bike seemed to leap forward, and Nadine was gripped more by excitement than fear.

There was definitely something exhilarating about the throb of the powerful engine beneath her, the speed and, yes, she had to admit it, the feel of a male body so close to her own.

They roared through the night for several miles, climbing, Nadine thought, although she couldn't be sure and she was too keyed-up to look.

It wasn't until Angelo brought the bike to a halt that she knew she had been right.

They were in a lay-by at the side of the road and, after Angelo had dismounted and helped her to do the same, Nadine saw that they were on the crest of the downs. Seeing that Angelo had removed his crash helmet, she did the same then, instinctively turning, she saw the lights of Hawksford far below and beyond them lights from other towns and villages in the surrounding countryside—some linked by glittering snake-like ribbons and others with great patches of darkness between.

The last quarter of the moon peeped intermittently from behind dark, scudding clouds and the chill April wind loosened tendrils of Nadine's hair, whipping them across her face.

'That wasn't so bad, was it?' Angelo was smiling at her, his dark eyes shining in the moonlight.

'No, I have to admit, it wasn't,' agreed Nadine.

'So, were you afraid?'

'No,' she said quickly and catching sight of his expression, added, 'Well, maybe a bit at first. . .but not afterwards. In fact, I found it quite. . .quite. . .'

'Exciting?' he murmured.

'I was going to say invigorating,' she replied coolly. It had been exciting but some inner voice of caution warned her not to admit that to Angelo.

'Maybe you will understand Paul now,' he said, and after a moment added, 'Maybe you will not be so hard on him.'

'I'm not hard on Paul,' she protested. 'I'm simply concerned for his safety.' She turned as she spoke,

walked the few steps to the fence that surrounded the
lay-by and stood, looking out over the surrounding
countryside. 'The night view is almost as good as the
day time one,' she observed after a while.

'Yes, it is.' Angelo moved to join her, standing behind
her but so close as to be almost touching. 'It reminds
me of home.'

'Home?' She half turned her head but found his face
so close to hers that she hurriedly turned back again.

'Yes,' he replied softly, and she recognised the tender,
almost caressing note that came into his voice whenever
he talked of his home. 'Around Rome we have seven
hills. The views of the city are magnificent—at night
as well as in the day.' He paused. 'You have been to
Rome?' he asked.

'No,' she replied, 'no, I've never been to Rome.'

'But you would like to.' It was more a statement than
a question but nevertheless seemed to require an answer.

'Wouldn't anyone?' She kept her reply light, almost
flippant.

'Maybe it could be arranged,' he said.

'I have Paul to consider,' she replied quickly. It was
an excuse, she knew, and she knew that Angelo knew
it. Paul was of an age where he would curtail little, if
anything, she might want to do.

'Paul could come too.' Angelo's reply was instan-
taneous, as if he had somehow engineered this
conversation, anticipating her replies and plotting his
own. 'He would love Rome,' he added. When Nadine
didn't reply he went on, 'It can't be easy.'

'What can't be easy?' Sharply she turned her head,
forgetting how close he was.

'Bringing up a boy on your own.'

'You've said that before,' she retorted, 'and I told you
then—we manage.' Once again his manner irritated her.

'A boy needs a father.' She felt, rather than saw, his
shrug. 'Especially during his teenage years.'

'That may be so,' she replied sharply, 'but there's not

a lot I can do about it.' She turned her head almost angrily back to the night-time view but this time, as she stared at it through unseeing eyes, the lights blurred into each other. How dared he criticise her situation?

They were silent for several minutes, during which the only noise was the sound of the wind on that lonely downs road. She should move away from him, she knew that, but somehow she seemed powerless to move, as if her feet were rooted to the spot.

Just as she was becoming uncomfortably aware of his nearness he spoke, breaking the silence between them.

'So, there is not anyone in your life at the present time?' he asked softly.

'Not really.' She gave a little shrug. 'At least, not in the way you mean,' she added. Just for one moment her mind flew to Seymour Russell, but her relationship with the consultant wasn't like that and she had certainly never considered him as a possible stepfather for Paul.

'I find that hard to believe,' Angelo murmured in her ear.

She turned her head and, finding his face again only inches from her own, she moved abruptly so that she now faced him—at the same time forcing him to step back.

'What do you find hard to believe?' she demanded.

'That there is no one!' he said softly. 'I thought you would have had admirers queuing up.' As he spoke his gaze roamed over her, just as it had done earlier that day when they had been talking in her office, and now, as then, Nadine found that her heart was beating so fast that it threatened to suffocate her.

'If you think that you are sadly mistaken.' She gave a short laugh, desperately hoping that she sounded casual but afraid that her voice was unnaturally shaky. 'I only wish it were so—but I should be so lucky.'

'I don't understand.' He frowned and even in the restricted light from the moon she could see the bewilderment in his eyes. 'You are a very lovely lady, Nadine,' he said.

'It's kind of you to say so,' again her tone was bright, forced, 'but in my experience men tend to lose interest when they find out a woman comes with a teenage son and, in my case, a mother as well!'

'You are. . .how you say it. . .putting yourself down?' he protested.

'No,' she laughed again, 'simply being realistic. Besides, I prefer to leave all that romantic nonsense to the youngsters. . .'

'But you are a young woman, Nadine— a young, beautiful woman with so much to offer. Any man would be fortunate. . .'

'Supposing that doesn't interest me?' she interrupted him. 'Supposing I'm quite happy without a man in my life?'

'I don't think that is so,' Angelo replied seriously. 'I think you would be very happy with a man in your life.' He stepped closer to her again as he spoke while she, in turn, tried to take a step backwards, only to find the top bar of the fence pressing into her back.

'Maybe.' She gave another attempt at a light laugh. 'But it would have to be the right man.'

'Of course.' He, too, laughed. 'For anyone it has to be the right person. My mother asks me when I am going to marry. Every time I go home she asks me. "Angelo," she says, "when will you settle down?"'

'And what do you tell her?' asked Nadine.

'I tell her, yes, yes, I will. But not until I find the right woman.'

'And this right woman—so far she has eluded you?'

'Yes,' he nodded. 'But I shall know when I find her. . . Just as you, Nadine, will know when you find this right man. . .' Leaning forward slightly, he put his hands on the fence at either side of her—imprisoning her in the circle of his arms.

Aware that her heart was hammering harder than ever,

she stared at him, saw his expression soften in the moon-light and then fade into darkness as a cloud raced across the face of the moon.

Then, before she knew what was happening, he took her upturned face between his hands and, while gently caressing her jaw with his thumbs, allowed his fingers to become entangled in her hair.

She was helpless in his grasp, his powerful leather-clad figure blocking her escape, the solid wooden fence behind her and the loneliness of the downs all around them.

She felt a twinge of alarm, quickly followed by a sudden surge of panic. Had she been a fool to agree to this ride? It had all seemed innocent enough at the time but who would hear her up here, miles from anywhere, if she was to need help? What if Angelo's motives were less than honourable? What did she really know about this man who, after all, was practically a stranger?

Even as the thoughts flew through her mind his face came closer to her own. She tried to twist her head away, but he held her face imprisoned between his hands and there was no escape.

Angelo's mouth closed over hers, stifling the protest which had risen in her throat.

Her body stiffened in defence and instinctively she began to struggle but as she attempted to push him away he released her head and brought his arms round her once again holding her captive against the fence.

In the time that it took for Nadine to calculate what her next move should be something changed. His kiss grew demanding and, parting her lips with his tongue, more tender until Nadine——far from wanting to fight him off——to her horrified amazement found herself not only enjoying it but actually wanting more.

These were not the actions of an attacker——a potential rapist——this was something quite, quite different.

As if they had a will of their own, her arms crept up around his neck just as, from somewhere deep inside, she felt a leap of desire—a sensation almost forgotten by Nadine in recent years.

'Maybe,' he murmured softly when at last he drew away from her, 'maybe we could both have just found that right person.'

His words seemed to jerk her back to reality. A reality that told her that what he was suggesting was quite impossible. How could she even entertain the idea— and with a man only about ten years older than her own son?

Abruptly she twisted her head away from him, but not before she had seen the puzzled look on his face.

'Nadine?' he said. 'I have upset you? Offended you?'

'No, Angelo,' she said, 'no... But what you just said is quite impossible.'

'But why? I don't understand. I think you like me; maybe if we get to know each other a little better... maybe we should go out together?'

'I don't think so, Angelo...' she began.

'You don't like me? Just now, when you kissed me, I could have sworn otherwise...'

'No, Angelo, it isn't that,' she said hastily. 'I do like you, really I do...'

'Ah, that is good.'

'But I just don't think we should pursue that type of relationship any further, that's all...'

'I cannot understand why.' He sounded genuinely puzzled. 'You say you like me. I certainly like you...I like you from the moment I saw you when you get angry with me for parking in your space. I say to myself, there is one very lovely lady. Then, when I get to know you more, I like you even better...'

'Angelo, we've only known each other a few days...' she protested.

'How long does it take?' He shrugged. 'When you meet someone it happens here.' He touched his heart. 'It doesn't need time...you just know.'

She stared helplessly at him, wondering what she

could say next—secretly appalled at what had just happened between them, not just at the fact that it had happened but that she had let it happen, and of the effect it had had on her.

Even as her mind raced, he lifted his hand and gently ran the back of his fingers down her cheek. Suddenly she was reminded of something Lee Bevan had said. Angelo had done that to her, and that had been just after he had kissed her. No doubt Karen Ashton had received the same treatment, as, probably, did every other girl who caught his fancy.

Nadine took a deep breath in a conscious effort to pull herself together. 'Angelo,' she said firmly, 'would you take me home, please?'

'But. . .' he began to protest but, pushing him aside, she strode back to the motorbike and picked up her helmet from the seat.

He stared after her for a moment then, with a sigh and a little shrug, he followed her.

He paused before putting on his own helmet and, lifting the visor of hers, said, 'You are not angry with me?'

'No, Angelo,' she said, 'I'm not angry with you.'

And strangely, surprisingly, she wasn't, for in spite of her earlier irritation Nadine found that she was no longer annoyed with him and, while there could be no question of the type of relationship between them that he had suggested, she knew that their relationship had changed. In what way it had changed she wasn't entirely sure—she only knew it had.

A slightly subdued Angelo took her home then. Their arrival at Montague House coincided with that of Paul's, who had just returned from Scotty's house.

As Nadine climbed from the back of the motorbike and removed her crash helmet Paul stared in openmouthed astonishment.

'Mum?' he said, peering at her in the light from an overhead streetlamp as if he couldn't believe his eyes.

'What's wrong?' She answered Paul calmly enough but, inside, her heart was still thumping uncomfortably. 'I think I've seen everything now,' said Paul. 'First Gran and now you.' He grinned at Angelo. 'I've got to hand it to you,' he said. 'I didn't think anyone could ever persuade Mum onto a motorbike.'

Without a word Nadine put her head down and, not daring to look in Angelo's direction, she hurried into the house. It was a good job that her son didn't know the full extent of Angelo Fabrielli's persuasive powers, she thought grimly as, without a backward glance, she made her way upstairs to the sanctuary of her flat.

Angelo settled easily into life at Acacia Avenue and into his job at the Spencer Rathbone. At home Nadine could not help but notice the easy camaraderie between him and Paul and the friendship that quickly grew between himself and Fee.

For her own part, while being polite and friendly towards him, she did nothing that he could possibly misconstrue as being encouraging. Reluctantly she had gradually been forced to admit that, in spite of her earlier protestations to the contrary, she did indeed find him attractive.

But at least she'd recognised the danger and was ready to be on her guard whenever he was around. There was simply no way that she could ever allow a relationship to develop between them. If she'd been ten years younger it might have been a different matter but she wasn't, and an affair with the young Italian quite simply was the last thing she wanted to happen.

On the ward Karen and Lee continued to be at logger-heads with each other as they vied for the registrar's attention, while Angelo appeared to treat them all in the same way—even Ruth, who seemed to blossom under the unaccustomed flattery.

He made no further reference to the moonlight ride he and Nadine had shared or to what had happened between them, continuing to treat her with the same courteous respect as he had before.

In the end she was forced to wonder if she had dreamt the incident—whether that brief flare-up of passion between them had simply been a figment of her imagination or whether, in fact, her first assumption had been correct and that it had indeed been his usual line of approach to any woman who happened to take his fancy.

The busy ward routine continued for the rest of the week, with Peggy Simpkins and Cyril Norman continuing to recover and Josh Barnes responding well to the new pin which had been inserted in his thigh.

Jennifer Dickinson was in much pain and discomfort following the removal of her disc, which had not proved to be as straightforward as Seymour Russell had predicted.

Bob Jenkins also had a traumatic week, suffering much pain from his pelvic injuries, but Barry Fletcher at last began to show gradual signs of recovery from his spinal fusion and started to respond to physiotherapy.

By the time the week was over Nadine was quite exhausted, and looking forward to some time off.

On the evening that Seymour Russell called to take her to the theatre Fee had already left the house to go to yet another rehearsal, while Paul and Scotty were deeply engrossed in a computer game.

Angelo had gone out, Nadine had seen him leave the house some half an hour previously. Idly she had found herself wondering where he was going, then had sternly dismissed the thought. It was nothing whatsoever to do with her what the new lodger did on a Saturday night or with whom.

'Nadine, you look charming,' said Seymour as he held the car door open for her.

With a contented little sigh Nadine settled into her seat. She had been looking forward to the evening and had taken trouble over her appearance, choosing a black two-piece in soft jersey with a long skirt and fitted jacket. She had draped a beige chiffon scarf around her neck, tossing one end over her shoulder, while her ash-blonde hair had been secured with a diamanté clasp. The overall effect was both elegant yet understated and one of which she knew Seymour would approve.

Nadine enjoyed Seymour's company. He was safe and predictable, if a little staid, but at least Nadine knew that she could relax with him; knew where she stood. There would be, she thought grimly, no wild night rides with a leather-clad Latin lover who gazed deeply into her eyes, kissed her hungrily and resurrected disturbing emotions which had died long ago and which she had imagined had been buried for ever.

They drove through the town towards the riverside theatre, their conversation light and of hospital affairs, then, as Seymour parked the car in the car park, he said, quite casually, 'I saw young Fabrielli just now down in the precinct on that monster of a machine of his.'

'Really?' Nadine involuntarily stiffened at the mention of Angelo's name.

'He certainly doesn't waste any time where the female members of staff are concerned, does he?' Seymour chuckled and Nadine threw him a sharp glance.

'What do you mean?' In her attempt to appear casual she feared that her voice sounded tight and brittle.

'Young Karen Ashton was getting on the pillion,' Seymour replied. 'That auburn hair of hers is unmistakable.'

Nadine opened the car door and stepped out. So that was where he had gone—out with Karen again.

They made their way into the theatre, and she found herself wondering if they had gone to the sports centre for their return squash match.

Not that it was of interest to her, of course, what Angelo did or with whom, she told herself firmly as Seymour bought programmes.

On the other hand, maybe they'd gone somewhere else—for a meal perhaps, or maybe he had simply taken

Karen for a ride—a ride through the night and up onto the downs to see the lights. . .

She struggled to dismiss the thought but as they took their seats in the theatre and the lights dimmed, to her acute annoyance, Nadine found that she couldn't get Angelo and Karen out of her mind. An image of the two of them kept flashing before her eyes with the girl on the back of the motorbike, her red hair flowing from beneath the rim of the crash helmet—the same helmet that she, Nadine, had worn.

Had he told Karen to put her hands inside his jacket to keep them warm as he had told her to do?

What if he had? What could it possibly matter to her?

Angrily she attempted to turn her attention to the play. It was Shaw's *Pygmalion*—usually a favourite of hers—but, for some reason, tonight she found it almost impossible to concentrate.

There was an excellent cast, who would shortly be taking the production to the West End, and desperately Nadine tried to focus her mind on what Eliza Doolittle was saying.

But only moments later her mind wandered again—this time to a vivid picture of Angelo and Karen together in some cosy restaurant, sharing a meal and a bottle of wine.

The images persisted throughout the play until, in the end, Nadine found it difficult to distinguish between Higgins and Eliza and Angelo and Karen.

At last, mercifully, the curtain came down for the interval and Seymour leaned across to speak to her.

'Superb cast,' he murmured, 'don't you agree?'

'Oh, absolutely,' she replied hastily, at the same time hoping that Seymour wouldn't go into any of the finer points of the production and asking her opinion as he usually did.

Somehow she got through the second act, but she was angry—angry with Angelo who somehow, albeit unwittingly, had ruined her evening.

And even after a light supper, while Seymour drove her home, she still found herself wondering.

Had Angelo taken Karen home? Would she have asked him in? Were they, even now. . .?

By the time they reached Acacia Avenue her nerves were stretched to screaming point and it came as quite a shock to see the Harley Davidson parked quietly in the drive in its usual place.

There was no sign of Angelo Fabrielli, Karen Ashton or anyone else, for that matter.

Seymour switched off the Wolseley's engine, and Nadine suddenly remembered her manners.

'Would you like coffee, Seymour?' she asked, at the same time hoping that he would decline.

'That's very kind of you, my dear, thank you,' he said, and her heart sank. Suddenly all she wanted was to get to bed.

The hall and landing lights were still burning but the rest of the house was quiet, and Nadine guessed that Fee had gone to bed. Likewise, when they passed Angelo's room there was no sound and when they reached her flat it was to find that Paul also had gone to bed.

Leaving Seymour browsing through her CD collection, Nadine made coffee in the kitchen and then carried the tray back into the sitting-room.

'How is your mother?' asked Seymour as she set the tray down on a low table.

'She's well,' Nadine replied. 'Very busy at the moment, of course, with rehearsals for the new Gilbert and Sullivan.'

'That opens soon, doesn't it?' Seymour took the cup she offered and sat down in an armchair, settling himself comfortably and crossing his legs.

'Yes, in a couple of weeks,' Nadine replied, picking up her own cup and sinking down onto the sofa. 'Mum will no doubt be arranging an opening night party— would you like to join us?'

'I should love to, thank you.' Seymour smiled, and it suddenly struck Nadine how tired he looked.

They sat and talked for a while then, after a second cup of coffee, Seymour sighed and stood up. 'I'd best be hitting the road,' he said. 'It's been a long week.'

She, too, stood up and followed him to the door, which he opened. 'Don't come down,' he said, 'I'll see myself out.'

'No, it's all right,' she replied quickly. 'I have to put the lights out. They were only left on for me.'

Quietly, so as not to disturb anyone, they descended both flights of stairs and as Nadine opened the front door Seymour paused then turned to her.

'Thank you, Nadine,' he said, 'for a delightful evening.' Gently he drew her into his arms and she lifted her face for his kiss. A kiss that was warm but as gentle as his embrace. A kiss between friends, rather than between lovers. A kiss that bore not the slightest resemblance to the last kiss Nadine had received.

'Goodnight, Seymour, and thank you,' she said.

She watched as he walked down the path and got into his car. Then, as he drove away, she lifted her hand in farewell before quietly closing the front door and sliding the bolt.

She lifted her hand to turn off the hall light and then froze, her hand still on the light switch.

Angelo was standing on the landing watching her.

CHAPTER EIGHT

BY THE time Nadine was halfway up the stairs Angelo had turned and gone back into his room. When she reached his landing his door was firmly shut.

She paused for one moment, staring at it.

Had he seen Seymour kiss her? It was more than likely that he had. But what of it? She gave a little shrug and carried on up the stairs to her room.

It shouldn't matter to her if Angelo had seen—after all, it was none of his business—who she chose to go out with or who she let kiss her. He'd been out with Karen Ashton that evening and she hadn't been bothered by that—hadn't even given it a second thought.

Opening her flat door, she stepped inside and, with one last glance through the bannisters at Angelo's closed door, deliberately with a loud click she shut her own door.

Suddenly she felt unbearably weary; the evening had not been what she had hoped and that had been no fault of Seymour's.

It had been her, and her inability to concentrate that had been the problem.

No doubt it was tiredness that was the cause, she told herself firmly as she prepared for bed, and all that was required to put that right was a good night's sleep.

The trouble was that, tired as she thought she was, sleep eluded her and she tossed and turned for hours and even when, eventually, she did drift off her dreams were so chaotic and muddled that she kept waking, and the whole exhausting cycle would start again.

*   *   *

111

In the morning she had difficulty remembering her dreams, but she had an uneasy feeling that Angelo had featured strongly in them.

As the early morning sunlight filtered through her curtains she lay in bed and found herself wishing, not for the first time, that Angelo Fabrielli had stayed in Italy; that he had never come to the Spencer Rathbone, and that he had certainly never come to stay in her home.

She still didn't know why she found his presence so disturbing; she only knew that just when she thought she was beginning to get used to his being around something else happened to upset her.

She must have drifted off to sleep again for when she awoke for the second time she saw it was nearly nine o'clock. She jumped, then remembered that it was Sunday and she was off duty. She yawned, stretched then got out of bed and padded to the door.

The flat was very quiet, which wasn't surprising for a Sunday morning, as Paul generally never surfaced much before noon.

On her way to the kitchen to make tea Nadine saw that Paul's bedroom door was open, and a glance inside showed his room to be empty—untidy, but empty.

Idly she wondered where he was, but it wasn't until she'd drunk her tea, showered, dressed and gone downstairs to collect the papers that she found out.

A delicious smell of fried bacon wafted up the stairs to greet her and she found Fee in her kitchen, breaking eggs into a frying-pan.

'Hello, darling,' Fee glanced up and smiled. 'Breakfast?'

'No, thanks,' Nadine pulled a face. 'I don't want to start that sort of bad habit.'

'Breakfast should be the most important meal of the day,' said Fee, manipulating the eggs expertly in the pan.

'That may be so, but I prefer to stick to my muesli and toast,' said Nadine, then with a frown she added, 'I didn't know you were into cooked breakfasts either.

You'd better watch it, otherwise you won't be able to get into your costume.'

'Oh, this isn't for me.' Fee looked horrified. 'It's for the workers.'

'Workers?' Nadine frowned. She hadn't heard anything about any workmen coming and, even if they were, Sunday was a funny day to start any repairs.

'Yes, out there.' Fee pointed to the window that overlooked the side of the house.

Curiously Nadine walked to the window and looked out.

She should have known really, she thought at the sight which met her eyes. A large tarpaulin littered with tools, buckets of water, sponges and other paraphernalia was spread across the path. Paul was washing the Harley Davidson while Angelo was crouching down, tinkering with something on the back wheel.

Paul saw her first and as he looked up the breath caught in Nadine's throat, and this time it wasn't because of the resemblance to his father but because it dawned on her that rarely had she seen her son looking so happy.

'Tell them their breakfast is ready,' said Fee as Nadine moved to the back door and into the conservatory.

'Hi, Mum,' said Paul. 'This is brilliant—it really is a fantastic bike.'

Nadine smiled, then found herself looking into Angelo's eyes as he moved out from the far side of the Harley.

'*Buon giorno*, Nadine,' he said quietly.

'Good morning, Angelo,' she replied, and would have turned away—gone back into the house—but something stopped her. Something in Angelo's eyes stopped her. Something which she was unable to define—some emotion, but whether it was a coolness or a question she had no means of knowing; she only knew that once again something had changed between them, just as it had on the night he had kissed her.

Only this time, as she collected the Sunday papers

and retreated back to her flat, she had the deflating
feeling that the change was somehow for the worse and
not, as it had been before, for the better.

This feeling of change persisted throughout the following week, both on the ward and at home. There was
nothing that Nadine could specifically put her finger on,
but it was there—a slight coolness between them as
subtle as a summer's breeze; a shift of balance.

And she found herself regretting it because she had
thought that after their disastrous beginning, they had,
perhaps, found a new understanding of each other.

But the problem now seemed to be that when he
wasn't around she wasn't able to get him out of her
mind—just like the evening at the theatre, he was
always there.

At home, she listened for his foot on the stairs, the
sound of his laughter as he shared a joke with Paul or
teasingly flattered Fee. If he was out she couldn't sleep
until she heard the Harley return. She might have spent
the entire evening wondering where he was and with
whom, but at least when he came home she knew that
he was safe and under the same roof as her. Only then
was she able to sleep.

On the ward she found herself listening for the sound
of his voice, waiting for his arrival on the doctors' morning round or keeping one eye on the patients to see if
he was paying one of his unofficial, but frequent visits
to reassure or to boost morale.

She was at a loss to explain why she behaved in this
way, a way that was for Nadine, who had become so
independent, so uncharacteristic; she only knew that she
did, and was powerless to do otherwise.

So involved had she become with these thoughts and
emotions over the new registrar that she almost forgot
the associations between him and the other members of
her staff—to such an extent that it came as a shock one
morning when, just as the doctors began their ward

round, a furious argument broke out between Lee and Karen in the nurses' station.

The whole ward, including the doctors and the patients, heard Lee accuse Karen of being a slut and of throwing herself at anything in trousers. They also heard Karen's not-too-delicate response.

Seymour Russell, who witnessed the whole unfortunate incident, merely raised his eyebrows and peered at Nadine over his glasses. The gesture was sufficient to register his distaste and to show that he expected her to sort the matter out.

Both girls were despatched to the rest-room to cool down and to await a reprimand.

At the end of the doctors' round Nadine thanked Seymour and then, as the group of grinning doctors prepared to leave the ward, she turned to Angelo and quietly said, 'Dr Fabrielli, a word, if you please.'

Angelo followed her into her office where, after he'd closed the door on a hushed and expectant ward, he turned to face her.

He looked as casually handsome as ever—his dark hair tousled, the neck of his shirt unbuttoned beneath the open white coat and his stethoscope slung round his neck.

'Nadine?' His surprise at being summoned was there in the one word.

Nadine took a deep breath. 'Dr Fabrielli,' she began and, as his eyebrows rose at the formality of the address in spite of the fact that they were alone, she hurried on whilst her anger would still see her through, 'I'm sorry,' she said, 'but I really can't have any more of these disruptions on my ward.'

'I agree,' he replied, 'they do no one any good.'

'Well, I'm glad you agree!' she exclaimed, 'So, can I assume you will do something about them?'

'I am sorry, Sister Hadley,' Angelo replied, his tone faintly mocking now, 'but I can't imagine why you should think these distressing incidents have anything to do with me.'

She stared at him in growing exasperation. 'I've told you before, Dr Fabrielli,' she said, 'you seem to have an unsettling influence on my nurses.'

'Really?' Amusement was lurking now in the dark eyes.

'At least two of them seem to think they have some sort of claim on your affections. No doubt you have given them just cause for this,' she carried on rapidly, 'so I would be grateful if you could clarify the position with the concerned parties. Maybe then tensions will be resolved and we can all get on with our work.'

'I would be more than happy to do that to make life easier for you, Sister. . .'

'Fine. Thank you, Dr Fabrielli,' she interrupted crisply.

'That is. . .' he went on smoothly, 'if I were able to. Unfortunately, I think you will find there has been some sort of misunderstanding.' He was smiling openly now, the dark eyes full of amusement.

Nadine felt her annoyance rise. How dared he make fun of her and ridicule her attempts to impose discipline on her ward? 'No, Dr Fabrielli,' she said, holding onto her temper with difficulty, 'I don't think you will find there is any misunderstanding at all—all I am asking you to do is to sort things out between the two girls in question. . . Now, if you will please excuse me, I have a very busy ward to run.'

He stared at her for a very long moment, his expression changing from one of amusement to something else—something Nadine had difficulty in identifying until, without another word, he turned and quite casually strolled from her office.

Nadine watched him go, her senses in turmoil. Just what did he think he was playing at? It was quite obvious from the events of the morning that he was still stringing both Lee and Karen along.

Thank God, thought Nadine with a slight shudder, that she hadn't taken him seriously when he had suggested that they get to know each other better. It would have been so easy to agree, but to what end? Simply to become another statistic on his list of conquests for him to boast about to his friends when he returned home?

For one moment, as the door closed behind him, Nadine stood very still. The incident had upset her, there was no denying that, but she still had Lee and Karen to sort out and a hundred and one other jobs to do, so she made a conscious effort to pull herself together.

She was on the point of having Jayne send the two girls to her office when she thought better of it and instead decided to go to them in the nurses' rest-room. That would, she thought, save any further speculation on the ward, where staff and patients alike were still agog from the morning's events.

She found the girls yards apart and silent, Lee sitting at a coffee-table flicking angrily through the pages of a glossy magazine and Karen standing at the open window smoking a cigarette.

Nadine decided that her best course of action was to go straight to the point.

'I don't intend putting up with that sort of behaviour from either of you on my ward ever again,' she said quietly. 'I just wanted to make absolutely certain that you are both aware of that.'

'It wasn't my fault. . .' Karen swung from the window, grinding out her cigarette.

'Yes, it was,' snapped Lee. 'If you hadn't. . .'

'I don't care whose fault it was,' said Nadine. 'If it happens again I don't want either of you on my ward. This has been brewing for ages now, and I've been patient with you both. I'm not prepared to listen to any further excuses. Sort yourselves out and leave your personal problems at home in future. . .' She paused as the phone suddenly rang. Turning, she picked up the receiver.

It was Jayne.

'Sorry, Nadine,' she said, 'I've just had A and E on the phone. They've had an RTA and are sending up two patients within the next half-hour.'

'Right, thank you, Jayne,' she replied. 'We will be right with you.' She replaced the receiver and looked up at Lee and Karen. 'Come on,' she said, 'we're all needed.'

'I'm sorry, Nadine,' said Lee.

'Yeah, so am I,' mumbled Karen.

'Shall we say the matter is closed?' Nadine glanced from one to the other of the two girls, wondering fleetingly which of them Angelo would settle for. Then, as the two of them nodded, she put the thought out of her mind. It was no concern of hers which of these girls he wanted. Whatever decisions Angelo Fabrielli made about his love life really weren't of any interest to her. Then the moment was gone and they all made their way back to the ward.

The two patients involved in the same road traffic accident were an elderly man and a young boy. The man had sustained serious multiple injuries and the boy had head and spinal injuries. Both were to go to Theatre, where Seymour Russell was to operate on the boy and Tom Selby on the man.

'Do we know what happened?' Nadine asked Jayne, as Seymour and Angelo arrived on the ward to study the X-rays.

'Not entirely. . .' Jayne shook her head. 'The police are hovering. They want to question both patients but I told them they could have a long wait.'

'I don't like the look of this.' Seymour was peering at the X-ray of the boy's neck and upper spine. 'I think we could have problems here. Would someone get one of the neurosurgeons for me?'

'Did the boy go through a windscreen?' asked Angelo.

'According to the paramedics, yes,' replied Jayne,

studying the report from A and E. 'That would account for the mess his face is in.'

'Wasn't he wearing a seat belt?' asked Seymour.

'Doesn't look like it,' replied Nadine.

'So, the other patient, the gentleman. . .' Seymour turned his attention to the other set of X-rays '. . .was he the driver of the same vehicle?'

'No. . .' Jayne was still scanning the report '. . .according to this, he was a pedestrian.'

'I don't know who has the worse injuries,' mused Seymour, 'this man or the boy passenger.'

'Oh, the boy wasn't a passenger,' said Jayne, reading on. 'According to this, it looks as if he was driving the car that hit the pedestrian.'

'Driving?' Seymour and Angelo both swung round from examining the X-rays. 'How old is he, for God's sake? added Seymour.

'Fourteen,' replied Jayne grimly.

'Nadine.' Lee suddenly appeared. 'A relative of the boy has just arrived. She wants to speak to someone about his injuries.'

Seymour glanced at Angelo.

'I'll do it,' said Angelo. 'Where is she?'

'I've put her in your office, Nadine,' replied Lee.

As Angelo headed for the office and Seymour took himself off to Theatre to get scrubbed up Nadine hurried onto the ward to satisfy herself that both patients were ready for surgery.

She went to the man first, a Mr Albert Whittington, whose age from his date of birth she calculated to be seventy-eight. Apart from his more serious injuries to both legs, pelvis, one arm and a ruptured spleen, he had sustained much bruising and many lacerations. His pulse rate was slow, his blood pressure low and his complexion unnaturally pale.

Karen and Ruth were preparing him for Theatre— dressing him in the customary white gown but at the same time covering him with several blankets. 'He was

becoming hypothermic,' said Ruth, glancing up at
Nadine.

The old man's eyes were closed, his white hair ruffled,
but as Nadine leaned over him he briefly opened his
eyes and stared at her in bewilderment. 'Hello, Albert,'
she said gently.

'Where am I?' The watery blue eyes were blank.

'You are in hospital,' she said. 'You've been in an
accident.'

'I don't remember. . .' His gaze flickered as he spoke
and Nadine realised that Angelo had come to stand
beside her.

'Hello,' he said bending over the patient, 'we are
going to take you to Theatre to try to put you right.'

'My daughter. . .Mo. . .is she here?'

'Is she, Sister?' Angelo looked up and Nadine
glimpsed the compassion in his eyes.

'I'll go and find out for you.' It was Karen who
answered his question, before hurrying off down
the ward.

Mr Whittington closed his eyes again and, as Ruth
continued with her preparations, Nadine and Angelo
moved to the boy's bed. He, too, had suffered many
cuts and much bruising to his face, and his neck was
supported by a brace. The area around both eyes was
so swollen that it was difficult to tell whether his eyes
were open or not.

A thin, anxious-looking woman was sitting beside his
bed. She looked up quickly, expectantly, as Nadine and
Angelo stopped, almost as if she thought they could
perform some miracle and restore the boy to how he
had been when she had last seen him.

'This is Mrs York,' said Angelo. 'She is Simon's
mother.'

'Hello, Mrs York,' said Nadine. 'Dr Fabrielli will
have told you what is happening.'

The woman nodded, twisting her hands nervously in
her lap. 'He's got to go to Theatre. . .an operation. . .'

'That's right,' Nadine nodded, but before she could say more the woman said, 'He told me he wouldn't do it again; he promised me. . . I'd warned him; time and again I'd warned him. He got away with it before. . . Oh, the police had warned him once but he took no notice; said it gave him a buzz. . . Given him more than a buzz this time, hasn't it. . .?' She turned her head sharply to look at her son, and Nadine caught the gleam of tears in her eyes. Suddenly she felt sorry for the woman. It wasn't easy bringing up teenagers, as she knew only too well.

'He's broken his neck, hasn't he?' The woman looked sharply at Angelo.

'We don't know that, Mrs York,' said Angelo. 'Not for sure. We won't know until we get him in Theatre.' He glanced up as the sound of loud voices suddenly reached them.

'I'll go,' said Nadine, mindful of the earlier episode on the ward and not wanting a repeat performance.

But this time it wasn't the staff who were responsible for the commotion. Mr Whittington's family had arrived—his daughter, Mo Ryan, her husband and an assortment of other people who might or might not have been their offspring. All were demanding noisily that they should be allowed to see Mr Whittington.

'Would you and your husband come into my office?' Nadine asked Mo Ryan. 'And the rest of you, please, would you wait outside?'

There were mutterings and murmurings from the others but eventually they complied with Nadine's request and then, as Mr and Mrs Ryan followed her into her office, she was joined once again by Angelo. She threw him a quick, grateful glance as he shut the door behind him.

'Now, Mrs Ryan,' Nadine briskly turned her attention to the couple, 'what did they tell you in A and E about your father's condition?'

'A and E?' said the woman blankly. 'What's that?'

'Casualty,' said Nadine.

'Oh, Casualty. Why didn't you say that? Well, they said he'd been run over by a car. Silly old devil, he was always wandering about. I was always telling him he'd get run over one day. Wasn't I always telling him, Sid?' She turned to her husband.

'Yeah.' Sid nodded. 'She were always telling him,' he said.

'So, how bad is he?' Mrs Ryan glared at Nadine as if this whole thing were her fault.

'Your father is very badly injured.' It was Angelo who answered and Mrs Ryan swivelled in her chair to look up at him.

'How bad is "badly", Doc?' asked Sid.

'He has broken bones, cuts and much bruising, and we fear there may be internal injuries,' Angelo replied.

'Oh, my Lord!' Even Mrs Ryan looked daunted at that.

'Unfortunately, your father's age isn't on his side either, Mrs Ryan,' said Nadine.

'Are you saying he might die?' asked Sid suddenly.

'She didn't say that,' said Mrs Ryan. 'You didn't say that, did you?' she demanded, looking at Nadine.

It was Angelo who came to her rescue. 'What Sister Hadley was saying,' he said patiently, 'is that your father's injuries. . .they are very serious, and. . .at his age any form of surgery carries a risk.'

'But you'll do what you can, won't you, Doc?' said Sid anxiously.

'Of course we will,' said Angelo. 'Mr Whittington will be going down to Theatre very shortly.'

'I want to see him first.' Mo Ryan struggled to her feet.

'I'm sure that can be arranged. Sister?' Angelo looked at Nadine who nodded and crossed to the door, opening it and calling to Enid.

'Would you take Mr and Mrs Ryan to see Mr Whittington, Enid?' Nadine asked and, when the support

worker nodded, she ushered the pair from her office.
When they had gone she closed the door and, just for
one moment, leaned against it.

'Phew!' she said, closing her eyes.

'I think,' said Angelo softly, 'you are having what
you call quite a day.'

'Yes, you could say that!' She opened her eyes and
gave him a wry smile. 'I only hope I'm not around when
Mr and Mrs Ryan discover that not only was their father
run over by a joyrider but that the joyrider is also a
patient on the same ward.'

'I fear you could have the Third World War on your
hands.' Angelo laughed then, glancing at the clock on
the wall, he added, 'I, too, will be in trouble if I don't
get down to Theatre and get scrubbed up.'

He turned to go, but Nadine stopped him. 'Thanks
for your help, Angelo,' she said quietly.

'It was nothing.' He shrugged.

'No, really, I mean it. Very few registrars are as
thoughtful as you.'

'I think it is the least I can do after this morning. . .'

'I thought you said that wasn't your fault,' she said
quickly.

He had turned to the door but he paused, one hand
on the handle, then he turned and looked at her. 'It
wasn't,' he said briefly. 'I say it was the least I could
do only because you thought it was my fault.'

Then he was gone, leaving Nadine staring after him
with a puzzled frown on her face.

The day continued in the same frantic vein. Albert
Whittington went to Theatre, where Tom Selby and his
team did their best to repair his shattered body, then he
was returned to the orthopaedic ward to recover.

'He's very frail,' Ruth told Nadine later in the day
after she had carried out a series of routine observations.

'Dr Selby has said we can increase his analgesics if
necessary,' replied Nadine, studying Albert's chart.

'Good.' Ruth nodded, then added, 'He's also been vomiting; can we give an anti-emetic?'

'I'll check for you,' said Nadine, picking up the phone. 'We have to bear in mind that he is also suffering from rheumatoid arthritis and he takes anti-inflammatory drugs.'

They had barely got Albert comfortable when Simon York came back from Theatre.

'The good news,' said Angelo, who accompanied the boy onto the ward, 'is that his spinal cord is intact.'

'Well, thank God for that,' said Nadine, watching as the porters transferred the boy from trolley to bed.

'He's fractured his clavicle and his left tibia and his face is in a bit of a mess,' said Angelo, 'but there's nothing that won't mend.'

'He's in better condition than poor old Albert,' replied Nadine grimly.

'Simon is young, but Albert's age is against him,' said Angelo, turning to look at the old man who appeared to be one mass of tubes and drips.

'Talking of age,' said Nadine, suddenly remembering something, 'Cyril Norman and Peggy Simpkins were due for discharge this afternoon. Cyril asked us to thank you and to say goodbye, but Peggy is refusing to leave until she's seen you personally.'

'In that case, I'd better go and see her.'

Angelo made his way down the ward to the ladies' section, and Nadine could not help but think how popular he had become in the short time he had been with them. He had a way with him that seemed to charm everyone, staff and patients alike.

If only he didn't have the power to cause so much disruption as well, she thought as with a sigh she turned away from the ward and went back to her office.

CHAPTER NINE

AT THE end of the shift, while Nadine was changing out of her uniform, Jayne asked her if she would care to go for a quick drink in the hospital social club before going home.

Nadine hesitated for a moment, then remembered that Paul had a sports meeting that night at his school and Fee had a dress rehearsal.

'I'd love to,' she said. 'I need to unwind after the day we've just had.'

The club was almost empty but, while Jayne was at the bar buying their drinks, Nadine was surprised to see Lee Bevan come in with the young paramedic whom she had at one time been dating. She smiled and waved at Nadine, then the pair of them went and sat in a huddle in a far corner of the bar.

'Talk about the resilience of the young,' sighed Nadine as Jayne returned and set their drinks on the table.

'What do you mean?' Jayne flopped down onto a chair and with a sigh kicked off her shoes.

'Lee Bevan.' Nadine lifted her glass, 'Cheers!' She took a sip of her drink. 'Over there.' She inclined her head slightly towards Lee and her paramedic.

Jayne gave a surreptitious glance over her shoulder, before taking a sip of her own drink. 'I'm not with you,' she said, turning back to Nadine with a frown.

'Well, to have heard her this morning, you'd have thought she would never get over Karen pinching Angelo Fabrielli from her and now just look at her— all over that young paramedic again.'

'But that's what it was all about,' said Jayne blankly.

'What what was all about?' Nadine frowned and set her glass down.

'The row this morning,' said Jayne. 'Didn't you know?'

'Didn't I know what?' It was Nadine's turn to look blank. 'I'm sorry, Jayne, but I think I must be missing something here. I understood that dreadful exhibition on the ward this morning was Karen and Lee fighting over Angelo Fabrielli. Are you telling me I was wrong?'

'I'm afraid you're a bit out of date,' Jayne chuckled. 'Enid told me that the row was over our young paramedic friend over there.'

'So what did Angelo have to do with it?' At this point Nadine was totally bewildered.

'Nothing, as far as I know.' Jayne shrugged. 'It appears that Lee had started going out with Dean Gardiner again—you know they were once an item? Well, they got back together again, and apparently Lee caught Karen chatting Dean up again. There has always been rivalry between those two over their men but this time Lee saw red. Mind you, I can't say I really blame her, especially after that last business with Angelo— not that they should have rowed about it in the ward,' she added hastily.

'Anyway, that is what it was all about this morning— Lee telling Karen to keep her hands off young Dean over there.'

'I can't understand why Karen is after Dean Gardiner when she quite obviously has scored with Angelo. . .' mused Nadine.

'Oh, but she hasn't,' chuckled Jayne.

'What do you mean?' Nadine stared at her friend.

'Apparently, and again this is only Enid's gossip—' Jayne leaned forward in a conspiratorial way '—Angelo had already made it plain to both Lee and then to Karen that he isn't interested in any sort of heavy relationship.'

'But he'd dated both of them!' retorted Nadine.

'Only casually. It seems it was the girls who had got

carried away by the whole thing, not our Italian friend.'

'So, you're telling me that all that episode this morning had nothing whatsoever to do with Angelo?' In growing dismay, Nadine continued to stare at Jayne.

'That's right. From what he told the girls it seems he is already committed elsewhere.'

'Oh, my God!' Nadine put her glass down. For some reason that possibility hadn't occurred to her.

'What is it? What's the matter? Nadine?' Jayne frowned. 'I know you reprimanded Karen and Lee but it was no more than they deserved. You can't have that sort of behaviour on the ward in front of the patients and the doctors, no matter who it's over. . .'

'No, Jayne,' Nadine sighed, 'you don't understand. It wasn't only Karen and Lee I had a go at.'

'You mean. . .?' Jayne's eyes widened.

'Yes,' Nadine nodded, 'I tore Angelo Fabrielli off a strip as well.'

'Oh, no!' Jayne groaned. 'What did you say to him?'

'I accused him of disrupting my staff and I as good as told him to make up his mind which one he wanted so that the fighting and bickering would stop.'

'Whatever did he say?' Jayne was staring at her now in a kind of fascinated horror.

'He tried to tell me there had been some misunderstanding but I wouldn't listen. God knows what he thought of me, jumping to the wrong conclusions like that.'

'I shouldn't worry too much if I were you,' said Jayne, growing serious again. 'After all, it's not as if he wasn't chatting them both up at one time. Perhaps it'll teach him a lesson.'

'Maybe,' said Nadine, draining her glass, 'but I guess I owe him an apology. He even told me later in the day that it hadn't been his fault—that I had only thought it was his fault—and I still didn't believe him or listen to him.' She stood up and looked down at Jayne. 'Do you want another drink?'

Jayne shook her head. 'No, I must be getting home. I have to pick Reece up from the childminder tonight. John is working late.'

'Yes, I must get home too. Mum is so involved in her amateur operatics at the moment I guess cooking the supper will be down to me.'

'How's it working out with Angelo Fabrielli lodging at your place?' asked Jayne, as the pair of them left the club and began to walk to the car park.

'OK, really, I suppose,' Nadine heard herself say. How could she tell Jayne the truth—that ever since his arrival she hadn't been able to get him out of her mind? Jayne would think that she had completely flipped if she even hinted at such a thing.

'Enid reckoned all along he must have someone else,' said Jayne. 'She told Ruth it stands to reason he would, with his looks.'

'And what did Ruth say to that?' asked Nadine faintly. By this time they were approaching their cars, which were parked side by side.

'She seemed quite miffed,' Jayne chuckled. 'Poor old Ruth. Do you know, I really think she thought she was in with a chance where Angelo was concerned but, when you think about it, there's probably someone back in Italy. Let's face it, there's bound to be—he's so gorgeous. . . We should have all realised it.'

'Yes, you're probably right,' replied Nadine. 'But it still doesn't alter the fact that I owe him an apology.' She pulled a face and Jayne laughed as she unlocked her car.

What Jayne had said was not only probably right it was also so obvious that Nadine couldn't believe that it hadn't occurred to her before. If she really stopped to think about it, it really was inevitable that, with his looks, his personality and his wealth, he would be involved with someone. But miserable as that made her feel, what was mainly on her mind as she drove home was her conversation with him.

He'd done it again. Made her feel really silly. What

was it about this man, for heaven's sake? No doubt he
was even now laughing at all of them for being so silly
and naïve where he was concerned.

When she drew onto the drive at Montague House
the first thing she saw was the Harley Davidson.

So he was home. She decided that she would go and
see him straight away and get her apology over and
done with.

As she opened the front door she heard a door close
on the landing. The rest of the house was quiet, Fee's
kitchen door was shut, which meant that she was still
out. Not giving herself any more time to think what she
was going to say, Nadine hurried up the stairs and tapped
on Angelo's door.

He opened it immediately as if he had been standing
directly on the other side then stood there, looking at her.

The words she had prepared died on her lips as she
saw that he was wearing nothing more than the briefest
of towels around his waist. He had quite obviously just
come from the bathroom, and Nadine realised that that
must have been the door she had heard closing.

'Oh, I'm sorry!' she said. 'I didn't. . .'

'It's all right,' he said. 'Everyone was out, so I took
the opportunity to have a bath.' His hair was still wet
and even as she watched in fascinated horror tiny rivulets
of water ran down his neck and onto the tangle of dark
hair on his chest. Quite suddenly she felt ashamed that
he should have thought that he would have to wait to
use the bathroom until everyone else was out of the
house. Had she given him that impression? She shifted
uncomfortably on the spot.

'You wanted to see me?' His dark eyes glittered with
amusement.

'Yes. . .I . . . that is, I'll come back. . .' she half turned
away, disturbed by the sensations that were assailing
her senses at the sight of his near-naked body.

'No, no need,' he said swiftly, standing back for her
to enter his room. 'Come in, please.'

Still she hesitated, not sure she could cope with this—
not sure she even should attempt to—but Angelo, completely unperturbed as if it were an everyday occurrence
for him to entertain a lady in this way, reached out his
hand and, taking her wrist, drew her into the room and
shut the door behind her.

'Please,' he said, 'sit down.' He indicated the Lloyd
loom chair in the bay window. 'And if you will excuse
me just for one moment.' His white teeth flashed in a
smile and he crossed the room, then disappeared into
his shower unit.

Uneasily Nadine glanced round. Familiar as she was
with the room, it looked different now. It was Angelo's
room. His leather jacket hung on a hook behind the
door. His crash helmet was on the top of the chest of
drawers. A pair of shoes protruded from beneath the
bed, a framed photograph of a woman—his mother perhaps—and a small ornament stood on the dressing-table
and there were books beside the bed. It was intimate.
These objects said things about the man. Things she did
not know. She looked up sharply as he stepped back into
the room. He was wearing a bathrobe now—a white,
towelling robe, which seemed to accentuate his Latin
colouring even more.

'Sorry about that,' he said. 'I just thought it was too
good an opportunity to miss.'

'Angelo.' Nadine took a deep breath. 'I hope I didn't
give the impression you couldn't use the bathroom. . .'

'Of course not,' he said, then added, 'But you did
point out it was for everyone's use and it's not as if I
don't have my own shower.'

'I know, but so do we. . .' she trailed off.

'It's OK,' he shrugged then, as he perched on the end
of the bed facing her, his bath robe fell open—revealing
long tanned legs covered with dark hair. Quite suddenly
this was a new Angelo—different from the white-coated
registrar, different even from the leather-clad motorbike
fanatic. This was a virile, intensely masculine Angelo

and Nadine, in embarrassment, found herself averting her eyes.

'You wanted to see me,' he said again, softly this time, raising his eyebrows.

'Yes.' She took a deep breath and in a concentrated effort to keep her mind firmly on what had to be said, she went on, 'I think I owe you an apology.'

'An apology?' Even he looked surprised at that, the smile fading slightly. 'Whatever for?'

'This morning.' Nadine swallowed. 'The row on the ward.'

'Ah, that.' Angelo nodded and the smile returned. 'You were very angry, I think.'

'Yes, yes, I was,' she said quickly. 'I don't like that sort of thing on my ward, especially in front of the patients. . .'

'And Seymour,' said Angelo solemnly.

'What?' Nadine looked sharply at him, thinking for one moment that he was mocking her, but his expression was quite serious.

'Seymour,' he said. 'I would not think you'd want any disruption in front of him either.'

'Well, no. Quite.' She paused, her line of thought lost for the moment. Then, as Angelo patiently waited—his eyes not leaving her face for even a fraction of a second—she went on, 'The thing is, Angelo, I blamed you for the upset.'

'Ah, yes,' he agreed softly, 'you did, didn't you?'

'I didn't realise that it wasn't anything to do with you,' she said, attempting to explain. 'That it wasn't your fault. . .' she added, trailing off, finding the intensity of his gaze disconcerting.

'Even though I told you so?'

'I'm sorry?' She frowned.

'Didn't you realise it wasn't anything to do with me when I tried to explain?' His tone was very soft now and he leaned further forward so that he was only a few inches away from her.

'No.' She moved back slightly, sitting more upright in the Lloyd loom chair. 'I didn't know you weren't involved until Jayne told me, and that wasn't until the shift was over. I'm sorry, Angelo, I should have listened to you.' Briskly she attempted to get to her feet, but he carried on speaking as if she hadn't moved.

'So what did Jayne tell you?' There was curiosity in his eyes now. 'Did she know what the row was about?'

'Sort of.' Helplessly Nadine sank back into the chair. He quite obviously didn't intend to move and she didn't think she wanted to brush past his legs. 'It seems that this time Lee and Karen were squabbling over one of the paramedics,' she said.

'And you thought they were squabbling over me?' The amusement was back in his eyes now.

'Yes, I did, Angelo. But, let's face it, it wasn't too great a mistake. After all, it wasn't that long ago that they both were fighting over you!'

'How fickle the female heart can be.' Sadly he shook his head, but the merriment wasn't far from his eyes.

'You're a fine one to talk,' she retorted, 'and you were dating them both, Angelo!' This time she did succeed in standing up. She didn't attempt to brush past him, however. She just stood, looking down at him and waiting for him to move.

He didn't immediately but continued to gaze up at her, while she found his close proximity even more disturbing. He had obviously just used some musk-scented preparation and it tantalised her senses. At least she thought it was that, but the longer she stood there the more she began to wonder if it wasn't his own scent—the purely male scent of him—that was affecting her.

'So, what else did Jayne tell you?' he asked at last.

Nadine hesitated, then said, 'Only that rumour has it that you must be committed elsewhere...'

'Really?' He looked surprised. 'And why should they think that?'

'Probably because you made it plain to both Lee and Karen that you didn't intend dating either of them again. . . Honestly, Angelo,' she said in growing exasperation, 'I don't know. Now, if you'll excuse me, I have to go.'

'Why?' he asked, without moving.

'Why?' She gave an incredulous little laugh.

'Yes, why do you have to go? It is pleasant sitting here talking to you.'

'I have things to do,' she protested. 'Besides. . .' she paused '. . .I'm not sure I should be here in your bedroom. . .like this. . .' Her gaze flickered over him. 'Whatever would people think?'

'People? What people?' Still he didn't move.

'Well, my mother—for a start!'

'Fee is not in,' he replied calmly.

Just for one second Nadine felt as she had on that lonely road that night when she had realised that she was alone with him, miles from anywhere. . . The only difference was that this time she didn't feel panic—only a sudden powerful throb of excitement.

'Besides,' he went on, 'I don't think she would raise any objection. . .'

'Maybe not,' Nadine replied wryly, 'but that's not the point. Come on, Angelo, really I do have to go.'

'Very well.' He sighed and stood up but still he didn't move. Instead he stood very still, looking down at her, while she found her gaze irresistibly drawn to his mouth—the finely shaped upper lip, the full, sensual curve of the lower.

The last time she had been this close to him he had kissed her; had stirred up all kinds of passions and emotions. She mustn't let that happen again. . .she hadn't got over the last time.

'Have you changed your mind yet?' Angelo murmured softly, his gaze roaming over her face, her hair. 'Have you decided you would like to get to know me better, after all?'

He was so close that she could almost feel the touch of his skin against hers; could anticipate the sweet, penetrating quality of his kiss once more.

Maybe. . .maybe. . . Just once wouldn't matter. Who would know?

She lifted her face. . .her lips parting slightly. . .her pulse racing.

'M-u-m!' The familiar shout echoed through the house. As Nadine drew sharply away she distinctly heard Angelo's sigh.

She only had time to wrench open the door before Paul bounded up the stairs. He stopped on the landing, his surprised gaze moving rapidly from herself to Angelo standing behind her in his bathrobe.

No one spoke then Nadine, only too mindful of how it must appear to Paul, ushered him up the stairs to their own flat without so much as a backward glance at Angelo.

As she shut the door behind her and Paul turned she held up her hand. 'Before you say a word,' she said warningly, 'that was not what you are thinking.'

'How do you know what I'm thinking?' Paul's eyes widened innocently.

'I know exactly what you are thinking,' said Nadine, 'and you can forget it. I know how that must have appeared, but I can assure you it was nothing of the sort. I went to see Angelo about something that had happened at work. . .'

'You don't have to explain, Mum,' Paul grinned. 'I quite understand. . .'

Nadine threw him a sharp glance. 'Well, just as long as you do.'

She hurried through to her bedroom, where she made a great show of hanging up her jacket and taking off her shoes—but her mind was racing.

She had seen the expression on Paul's face when she had opened Angelo's bedroom door, and it was one she hadn't seen on her son's face before—one that possibly signified that he had left his childhood behind.

And it had bothered her, more than she cared to admit it had bothered her. It had been just her and Paul for a very long time now. She had always known that one day that would change; that one day he would find a girl, marry and have a family of his own. But what she had seen in Paul's eyes had been something else, something that made her wonder if he had ever contemplated the reverse happening—contemplated losing her.

And it was all so unnecessary. There was nothing between herself and Angelo Fabrielli, and there never would be. Maybe he had been a pleasant diversion for a while. . .had rekindled old desires. . .but that was all it was. Soon he would return to Italy where, as they had already concluded, someone would be waiting for him. He would forget England, and the nurses he had flirted with; he would forget her.

She had to make Paul understand that, she thought desperately as she drew her hairbrush through her hair. Heaven only knew what he thought had just happened in Angelo's bedroom.

At a sudden sound she looked up sharply and in the mirror saw Paul, standing in the doorway of her bedroom.

'Paul. . .?' she began.

'I was just thinking,' he said.

'What about?' She turned to face him.

'That I was right,' he said. 'When I said that Angelo fancied you. . . You laughed at me, Mum, but I was right—I reckon he does fancy you.'

That night sleep once again proved to be a reluctant companion as the events of the day teemed through Nadine's brain, and it was well into the early hours before she finally drifted off.

She slept heavily, oversleeping and waking exhausted and with a niggling headache. She had just come to the conclusion that the day could only get better when she found that her car wouldn't start. In growing frustration she once again turned the key in the ignition.

'You have a problem?' She looked up to find Angelo, looking into her car, a concerned expression on his face.

She wound the window down a few inches. 'I think the starter motor has jammed,' she said.

'Let me try,' he said, standing back as she got out of the car.

He got into the car and tried the ignition, but once again the engine refused to come to life. 'You're right,' he said, 'it really is stuck.'

'I'll have to call the garage.' She glanced at her watch, then added, 'But I can't wait for them, I'll be late.'

'I'll give you a lift,' said Angelo, getting out of her car.

'Oh, there's no need,' she said quickly. 'I expect I can borrow Mum's car.'

'Fee says she's going into town shopping,' said Angelo quickly. 'She will need her car. No, come on, you come with me on the bike.' He grinned, his gaze meeting hers. 'You know what to do now, and you aren't afraid any more.'

'I wasn't afraid in the first place,' retorted Nadine.

'Good, so there is nothing stopping you.' He walked to the motorbike and took the now-familiar crash helmet from the pannier and handed it to her.

Her heart sinking, Nadine took it from him and eased it onto her head. She had no choice, really, she told herself as she watched him don his own helmet, mount the bike and ease it forward off its stand. If she didn't want to be late for her shift she had to accept his offer.

'You know the routine,' he shouted, lifting his visor.

She approached the machine and realised that, yes, she did now know the routine. Carefully she mounted, placing her hands on Angelo's shoulders just as he had told her to do before. Again she wore no gloves so, as her arms crept around his waist, she automatically tucked her hands inside his jacket for warmth.

And suddenly she was overwhelmed by how familiar and how right it felt to be sitting there, snugly fitted against his back, the smell of him in her nostrils—a mixture of his aftershave, of leather and that other, elusive scent that she had already come to recognise—the scent that was the very essence of him.

When they reached the Spencer Rathbone she found herself wishing that the ride had been longer as she realised just how much she had enjoyed it. And even when other members of staff, Ruth Stannard and Enid Farrow amongst them, saw her dismount, take off her crash helmet and shake out her hair she didn't care because, quite suddenly, it no longer seemed to matter.

She wasn't sure exactly what had happened to her or when; she only knew that something, yet again, had changed. She was unable to put her finger on what it was; she only knew that somehow her relationship with the young Italian had entered yet another phase. She wasn't even sure that she wanted to analyse it. She knew that she would have to and—soon, if the look in Angelo's eyes as he'd helped her to dismount had been anything to go by.

He had already made it plain that he wanted more to come of their relationship; to get to know her better, he had said, and even Paul had seen it and didn't seem to mind.

But, Nadine thought as she watched him walk away to the doctors' staff-room, what of the age difference between them? That hadn't changed. That was still there. It didn't seem to bother Angelo; did it still bother her? And what of the other person—the other commitment in his life which had been mentioned? The girl who, no doubt, waited for him in Italy? She wouldn't just disappear overnight even if other anxieties did.

When she reached the ward Nadine found that she had to make a determined effort to put all these thoughts out of her mind and concentrate on the job that had to be done.

Albert Whittington was very poorly that morning, after spending a bad night. The houseman had been called twice to deal with renal problems and a definite deterioration in Albert's general condition following his appalling injuries. He had not responded well to surgery, and by the time Nadine took over from the night sister he was suffering problems with his breathing.

'He's started a course of antibiotics but it looks as if bronchopneumonia is setting-in,' Nadine said to Jayne as they prepared their patient care plan for the day. 'I think we should inform his daughter. She asked to be kept informed of any change in his condition.'

'Right,' said Jayne, making a note on her pad, 'I'll give her a ring. What about young Simon York this morning?'

'There seems to be a problem with his left eye.' Nadine quickly scanned the boy's notes. 'The SHO wants the ophthalmic registrar to take a look at him. Apart from that, he seems to be responding well to treatment.' She paused and flicked through her records again.

'Jennifer Dickinson is making good progress, although she seems to be having constipation problems—probably due to the amount of analgesics she's taking. Her lactulose medication is to be increased. . . Josh seems much more comfortable now and doesn't seem to have rejected his new pin. . . Oh, and today is Barry Fletcher's big day.'

'Yes, I know,' Jayne smiled. 'Hans van Orden is coming up after doctors' round to get him out of bed.' She paused. 'We've also got three new admissions this morning and a full theatre list, so we've no time to hang around. . . Oh, by the way,' she said as she reached the door and looked back, 'what's all this I hear about our new ton-up sister?'

' "Ton-up sister"?' Nadine looked up blankly and,

as she caught sight of Jayne's amused expression, to her
annoyance she felt colour touch her cheeks. 'Oh, that,'
she shrugged dismissively. 'He gave me a lift in to work,
that's all. My car wouldn't start.'

'Oh, I see,' said Jayne innocently, 'that's all it was,
was it? Enjoy it, did you?' she added casually.

'It wasn't a question of enjoying it,' Nadine retorted
defensively. 'It was simply a case of getting to work. I
was grateful he was around, otherwise I would have
been late.'

'Quite,' said Jayne. 'But did you enjoy it?'

'Well. . .' Nadine began.

'It's a magnificent machine,' said Jayne.

'Yes, yes, it is,' agreed Nadine.

'Did he go really fast?'

'No, not this time. . .'

'Oh, so this wasn't the first time?' The question was
innocent enough but Nadine wished that she hadn't said
anything. She knew that however she tried to explain
that she had been on the Harley before it would be
misconstrued.

'I have been on it on one other occasion,' she admitted at last.

'That's quite something for you, Nadine,' said Jayne,
'with your aversion to motorbikes.'

'I know,' agreed Nadine, 'but I've come to realise
you can't blame the bikes for what happens—it's all
down to the rider,' she added seriously.

'Is that so?' Jane grinned.

'So Paul tells me,' added Nadine hastily.

'So, he's good, is he?' Jayne was still grinning.
'Angelo, I mean?'

'He seems to be, yes,' replied Nadine primly. 'Jayne,
we must get on,' she said briskly, standing up and
moving out from behind her desk. 'The doctors will be
here before we know where we are.'

'Yes, of course.' Jayne opened the office door and
stood back for Nadine to precede her. 'I take it you'll

be repeating the experience, then,' she said as they walked out onto the ward.

'What do you mean?' Nadine threw her a startled glance.

'Another motorbike ride,' said Jayne.

'Oh, I don't know about that,' replied Nadine, hoping to scotch the rumours she felt sure were about to start.

'Well, if he brought you to work, one hopes he is intending to take you home as well,' said Jayne.

'Yes, yes, of course,' said Nadine, an impatient note creeping into her voice. 'Yes, I dare say he will. Now, are you going to go and make those phone calls, Jayne,' she went on briskly, 'or do I have to do them myself?'

'Oh, I'm going,' said Jayne with another grin. 'Don't worry, I'm going.'

CHAPTER TEN

WHEN Albert Whittington's family arrived it soon
became apparent that they had discovered the true nature
of his accident and that it hadn't, as they had first
thought, been his own fault.

'Bloody joyrider,' said Mo Ryan in a very loud voice
to anyone who happened to be listening, and as it was
during doctors' round this proved to be to a fairly exten-
sive audience. 'That's what it was. Why they're called
joyriders beats me. I doubt whether my old dad would
see any joy in it.' She paused long enough to glance at
her father who, mercifully, was probably not even aware
of his daughter's presence or, for that matter, anyone
else's.

'I know what I'd do with him if I got my hands on
him,' Mo went on relentlessly. 'I'd string him up, that's
what I'd do,' she went on, just in case anyone was in
any doubt. 'Murderers—that's what they are. Cars are
just as lethal as guns when it comes down to it. That's
what I've always said. Isn't that what I've always
said, Sid?'

Sid, who was sitting on the opposite side of Albert's
bed from his wife, nodded. 'Yes, that's what you've
always said,' he agreed.

Nadine was standing with the group of doctors gathered around Bob Jenkins's bed discussing his progress.
Glancing at Seymour Russell, who was studying Bob's
records, she saw the frown lines on his forehead deepen
slightly.

'Can we do anything about this situation, Sister?' he
asked softly, his gaze flickering briefly from Mo Ryan
to Simon York, whose mother was seated by his bed.

The rest of the team might have assumed that

Seymour was referring to Bob Jenkins's situation, but Nadine wasn't in any doubt as to what he meant. She, herself, had been becoming increasingly aware of what Mrs York must be going through as she sat beside her son, well within earshot of Mo Ryan's observations.

'Maybe we could discuss it after your round,' she murmured in reply to Seymour's question.

By the time they moved away from Bob Jenkins's bed Mo Ryan had turned her attentions to Simon's mother.

'That your son, love?' she called across the ward, and when Mrs York half turned, giving only the briefest of nods in reply, she went on, 'He been in an accident too, has he? Poor lad. I know just how you feel. You feel so helpless. Don't you, Sid? Didn't I say that last night, Sid? Didn't I say you feel so helpless?'

'Yes, you did,' agreed Sid.

'Mind you,' Mo went on, 'I wouldn't feel so helpless if I could get my hands on the one who did this to my poor old dad. I expect you feel the same way, don't you, love?' she called to Mrs York.

'Something has to be done,' said Seymour a few minutes later as he and Angelo joined Nadine and Jayne in the office. 'I fear the consequences if that woman finds out. What is the situation with her father at the moment—he's Tom Selby's patient, isn't he?'

Jayne nodded and glanced through Albert's records. 'He's deteriorating quite rapidly,' she replied.

'So we could have the complication of his family having to cope with his death, combined with what may happen if they find out about young Simon York? Is that correct?' asked Seymour.

'Yes, that's correct,' Nadine nodded.

'Should the old gentleman not be moved to a medical ward?' asked Seymour, peering at them over his glasses.

'He should be,' agreed Nadine, 'but Medical is full at the moment.'

'May I make a suggestion?' Angelo had been browsing through Simon York's notes, but he looked up.

'Please do,' said Nadine. 'Anything. . .'

'I see young Simon has a possible eye infection, and is seeing the ophthalmic consultant today.'

'Yes. . .' agreed Nadine.

'Maybe, if they have room, we could move him to the eye ward?' Angelo looked from one to the other of them.

'I really need him here on Ortho,' mused Seymour.

'It would only be a temporary measure,' said Angelo. 'From what you say, Mr Whittington will not survive for very much longer so to avert what could be a nasty incident. . .?'

'I think it's an excellent idea,' said Jayne then, glancing at Nadine, she said, 'What do you think, Nadine?'

'It's up to Seymour really. Simon is his patient. Seymour? What do you say?' Nadine turned to the consultant.

'Yes, all right,' he nodded. 'Provided it's temporary and provided Ophthalmic can take him, of course.'

'I'll go and check,' said Jayne and then, as she reached the door and looked out through the glass partition onto the ward, she said, 'Oh, Hans van Orden's just arrived to help get Barry Fletcher out of bed.'

As Jayne hurried away Seymour said, 'I'll go and watch this as well—it's been a long haul for Mr Fletcher.' He was about to leave the room when he suddenly appeared to remember something and turned back. 'Nadine,' he said, 'I almost forgot—about Saturday?'

Only too aware that Angelo was listening to every word, Nadine said, 'Yes, Seymour. What about Saturday?'

'Isn't it the opening night of the Gilbert and Sullivan?' he asked, raising his eyebrows.

'It is indeed.' Nadine smiled. 'And I have our tickets—compliments of my mother.'

'Would you like me to pick you up?' asked Seymour.

'No, I'm on a late shift,' replied Nadine. 'I'll go straight to the theatre—I'll meet you in the bar.'

'Very well.' With a brief nod Seymour strode out of the office onto the ward, leaving Nadine with Angelo.

'This is Fee's big night you are talking about?' asked Angelo.

'Yes.' Nadine agreed. 'It's the biggest part she's had to date; it will be quite a moment for her—and for me!' she added. 'I get so nervous for her when she's performing.'

'And Seymour will be there to share it with you. . .' said Angelo softly.

There was a faint note of reproach in his voice and Nadine stiffened slightly. She couldn't cope with this. Not now. Not on top of all the other problems that the day seemed to be hurling at her.

'Yes,' she said as briskly as she could, 'Seymour loves the theatre. . .just as I do.' She paused. 'And, talking of big moments, I think I'll go and share Barry Fletcher's—are you coming?'

'Of course,' Angelo replied. 'I wouldn't miss it for the world.'

The section of the ward where Barry Fletcher's bed was seemed to have taken on something of a festive air as he prepared, with the help of the physiotherapist, to get up after the long spell he'd spent lying flat on his back and to walk his first steps since his spinal fusion.

Josh Barnes, who had been Barry Fletcher's companion for the duration of his stay, had asked someone to bring in a packet of coloured balloons. During the course of the morning Josh had blown up the balloons and attached them to the rail of his bed. Then as Barry, leaning heavily on a walking-frame, took his first faltering steps down the ward he was accompanied by the sound of erupting party poppers which Josh had persuaded Karen Ashton to distribute amongst the other patients.

Even Seymour Russell smiled at the impromptu celebrations and Nadine turned a blind eye to the noise and commotion, joining in herself with the spontaneous applause from staff and patients alike when a triumphant but desperately tired Barry returned to his bed at the end of the exercise.

'Well done, Mr Fletcher,' Seymour congratulated his patient. 'Another week should see you well on the road to recovery and the possibility of going home.'

'Nadine.'

Jayne touched her arm and Nadine turned swiftly to her senior staff nurse. 'What is it?' she asked.

'I've been onto the eye ward; they can take Simon York.'

'Good,' Nadine replied. 'Could you organise his transfer immediately, please, Jayne?' she said and, glancing at Angelo, she added, 'Dr Fabrielli, seeing this was your idea and you were so involved with Simon York's surgery, would you like to come with me and explain to Simon and his mother what is happening?'

As Seymour nodded in agreement Angelo followed Nadine down the ward to Simon's bed, where she drew the curtains to shut out the curious stares of Mo Ryan, Sid and two other members of the Ryan family who had just arrived.

Mrs York looked startled as her gaze fell on Angelo, and Nadine saw her anxiety. 'It's all right, Mrs York,' she said quickly, 'there's nothing to worry about. Dr Fabrielli has something he wants to explain to you both, that's all.'

'Mrs York, Simon.' Angelo gave his dazzling smile, the one Nadine used to think was purely for effect—designed to charm—but which she had come to realise was genuine, was purely Angelo—the way he was. 'We have decided,' he went on, 'to move Simon to another ward. Only for a short period of time,' he hastened to add as both he and Nadine saw the increased alarm on Mrs York's face.

'But why?' she asked, frowning. 'He's got used to it here now, haven't you, Simon?'

'I want to go home,' said Simon sulkily.

'Simon has been complaining of some pain in his left eye,' Angelo went on. 'We have arranged for an eye specialist to have a look at it.'

'An eye specialist!' Mrs York looked even more worried. 'But, before, you said it was only an infection.' She looked accusingly at Nadine.

'It may well be just that,' said Angelo calmly, 'but we need to be sure. So, what we are going to do is to take Simon down to the eye ward for a while, then, when we are certain everything is well with his eye, we will move him back here.'

'All right.' Mrs York nodded, then said, 'When are you going to move him?'

'Right away,' replied Nadine, drawing back the curtains as she spoke.

Mrs York suddenly grabbed her wrist, 'That man,' she said, her gaze flickering briefly in Albert Whittington's direction, 'how is he?'

'He's not very well, Mrs York,' said Nadine quietly.

'No, I didn't think he was,' she muttered.

Moments later, while Simon was being wheeled past Albert Whittington's bed by Nadine and Karen, Mo Ryan looked up. 'Going home, is he, love?' she called out.

It was Nadine who replied on Mrs York's behalf. 'No,' she said, 'Simon's only going to another ward, that's all.'

'Oh, poor lad,' said Mo. 'I hope he goes on all right, love. I really do. I know just how you feel. Victims, that's what they are—your lad and my old dad—victims. That's what I said, didn't I, Sid?'

Not waiting for the long-suffering Sid's reply, Nadine beat a hasty retreat.

*   *   *

Albert Whittington slipped into a coma about an hour
after Simon York's departure from the ward and died
during the afternoon. Angelo had been assisting
Seymour Russell in Theatre with a hip replacement, and
he'd just come to the ward to check on his patient who
had experienced respiratory problems during surgery.
He was in time to witness Mo Ryan's hysterics at losing
her father.

'May I talk to her?' he asked Nadine.

She nodded and, as Angelo disappeared into her office
to comfort Mo and Sid, Nadine slipped back inside the
cubicle where Karen and Enid were laying out the body.

'Poor Albert,' said Nadine, looking down at the old
man who looked calm and peaceful in death. 'No one
should have to end their life in that way.'

'That boy will be in trouble now,' said Karen.

'That's nothing to do with us,' said Nadine. 'That's
a matter for the police. Simon York is just as much our
patient as Albert was, and will receive the same care
and consideration.'

When Nadine eventually returned to her office she
found Angelo crouched in front of Mo—a red-eyed, now
strangely silent Mo—who was sitting in an armchair
drinking a cup of tea. Sid was standing by the window
smoking a cigarette. At any other time Nadine would
have asked that the cigarette be put out, but on this
occasion she remained silent.

'What do we do now?' asked Sid helplessly, turning
from the window.

Angelo stood up and, still looking down at Mo, he
said, 'You go home, Mr Ryan—to your family. You
take your wife home and comfort her, and your family—
they too will be in shock. They have lost their grand-
father.'

'I know.' Sid finished his cigarette and looked round
for somewhere to stub it out. Not finding anywhere, he
ground it out on the sole of his shoe. 'Come on, Mo,'
he said, 'it's time we went. We can't do no more here.

And what the doc says is quite right. We can't do no more for your dad now; we'd best get back to the kids. Thanks for everything, Doc, Sister.'

He nodded first at Angelo and then at Nadine and, crossing the office to the armchair, he put his hand beneath his wife's elbow and assisted her to her feet.

They were halfway across the floor when Mo suddenly stopped and, turning, looked back.

'It was him, wasn't it?' she said. 'That lad in the bed opposite? It was him who run Dad over, wasn't it?'

For one moment Nadine was lost for words. All their careful manipulation seemed to have been for nothing. If she admitted the truth there was no telling what Mo's reaction might be. If she wanted further discussion on the matter it had to be with the police and not with them. Nadine drew a deep breath but, while she was still searching for the right words, it was Angelo who came to her rescue.

'What makes you think it was Simon, Mo?' he said gently.

'I just know it was. There was something in his mother's eyes when they passed the bed—when you took him down to that other ward.'

'So, how do you feel about it?' said Angelo quietly.

'Dunno, really.' Mo shrugged helplessly. 'At first I thought I wanted to kill whoever had done it. . .'

'And now?' Angelo stared down at her.

'He's only a lad, isn't he?'

'Yes, Mo, he is,' Angelo agreed. 'What he did, on the other hand, was very serious and I'm sure the appropriate steps will be taken but, like you say, he is only a boy.'

'He's even younger than my Joe. . .isn't he, Sid? Younger than Joe?'

'Yes,' Sid agreed, 'he is.'

'It's best to let your anger go,' said Angelo. 'It only makes you feel worse in the end.'

'Yes. I s'ppose so.' Mo nodded. 'Easier said than

done sometimes, though. It's his mother I feel for. I
know. . . I've got three boys of my own and I know
only too well what they get up to. He could do with
a good hiding, that's what. But I don't suppose he'll
get one.'

'Maybe not,' said Angelo, 'but he does know what
he's done and he has to live with that for ever—I would
say that will be his real punishment.'

As the door closed behind the Ryans, Nadine turned
to Angelo.

'Thanks for that,' she said quietly. 'You did really
well there.'

He shrugged. 'I don't know about that. . .'

'You did—all that about letting anger go. I'm sure
you helped Mo with her grief.'

'Well, I hope so,' he smiled. 'It's true—anger is so
destructive to healing.'

'It's been a strange day,' she said. 'A day of tears
and of celebrations.'

'A bit like life, really,' he said and as they both sob-
erly considered what he had said he added, 'Come on,
I'll take you home.'

Nadine had forgotten for the moment that he was
taking her home and now, as he reminded her, she felt
an unexpected little surge of pleasure. The scene with
the Ryans had surprised her, giving her yet another
insight into this quite remarkable young man's personality.

For the rest of that week Nadine was aware of a slight
buzz of speculation amongst the rest of the staff. Her
lift to work on the Harley Davidson certainly hadn't
gone unnoticed, and remained a topic of conversation
for some considerable time.

What did amuse her were the differing reactions from
the various members of staff—amazement from Lee,
almost open hostility from Karen and a bland silence
from Ruth. Even Seymour seemed to have heard the

rumours for, when he greeted her in the theatre bar on
the opening night of *The Gondoliers*, he made some
light-hearted reference to her pillion riding.

The bar was packed that night—mainly with family
and friends of the cast, who were all celebrating the
show's opening. Seymour, resplendent in evening dress,
bought her a glass of champagne and as more and more
people packed into the bar Nadine looked anxiously
around.

'What's wrong?' Seymour frowned.

'I was looking for Paul,' she replied.

'Is he coming?' Seymour looked surprised. 'I
wouldn't have thought this was his cup of tea somehow.'

'It isn't, really,' Nadine admitted, 'but he always
comes to Mother's opening night.'

'That's nice.' Seymour smiled and then, looking
across the heads of the assembled throng, he said, 'There
he is, over there—by the door. Oh, he isn't alone either.'

Some sixth sense warned her, even before she turned,
who she was going to see.

Together with Paul, Angelo forced his way through
the crowd to her side. He, too, was in evening dress and
looked quite stunning, the crisp white frill of his dress
shirt a perfect foil for his tanned features.

Nadine felt as if her knees had suddenly turned to
water as his eyes met hers. She hadn't known that he was
coming. Paul hadn't said anything and neither had Fee.

'Nadine,' he said, 'you look beautiful.'

She had been forced to change at work before coming
straight to the theatre, and was wearing a full-length
cream dress in heavy chiffon. She'd had no time to do
much with her hair, and was wearing it loose so that it
fell softly onto her shoulders.

'I didn't expect to see you here,' she said weakly,
desperately wishing that his unexpected presence wasn't
having quite such a dramatic effect on her and trying
once more to dismiss it. She told herself yet again that
it was crazy—that nothing surely could ever come of it.

'I am Fee's guest,' he said quietly, before turning to Seymour who had been greeting Paul.

Fee had arranged for them to sit together in the front row of the dress circle and Nadine found herself seated between Angelo and Seymour, with Paul on Angelo's other side.

They were all aware that this was Fee's biggest role to date and, as the curtain went up and the expected first night nerves amongst the cast were quickly overcome, they settled down to enjoy the performance.

And it was wonderful. Quite wonderful. Fee was enchanting, captivating both her audience and her own private party, but as Nadine glowed with pride for her mother's performance she was only too aware that the magic of the evening had been heightened for her by Angelo's presence.

At the final curtain call, as the thunderous applause bought the audience to its feet, Nadine—completely overwhelmed by emotion—felt tears on her cheeks.

They all returned to Montague House, together with other members of the cast as Fee's guests for a first night party. Wine flowed and the house echoed with the sounds of music, sparkling conversation and much laughter.

To Nadine's amusement, Seymour appeared to be utterly entranced with Fee as she held court, laughing and talking with other members of the cast as they described near-disasters that had occurred during rehearsals.

'Mum—' Paul was suddenly at her elbow—'do you think Gran would mind if I went upstairs now?' he murmured anxiously.

'I'm sure she wouldn't,' Nadine replied, following him into the hall. 'I would say you've more than fulfilled your obligations.'

'Oh, it's not that,' said Paul hurriedly. 'I've quite enjoyed it all, actually, and I would stay, but England is playing Spain tonight and it's being televised.'

'Go on,' Nadine laughed. 'I'll cover for you, if need be.' She watched affectionately as her son disappeared up the stairs and as she turned to go back into the lounge she found that Angelo had followed her into the hall, and was also watching Paul.

'He has had enough?' he asked.

Nadine nodded. 'He'll do anything for Fee—he adores her—but there comes a time. . .especially when there's football on the television.'

Angelo smiled. 'I don't think Paul is the only one adoring Fee at the moment,' he said, glancing into the lounge where they could both see Seymour who was sitting on the sofa and gazing up at Fee with rapt attention.

Nadine gave a wry smile and raised one eyebrow.

'Do you mind?' Angelo asked quietly.

'Why should I mind?' she replied.

'Seymour was your escort tonight. . .'

'And you were Fee's special guest. . .' She gave a light shrug and would have gone back into the lounge but Angelo caught her arm. 'It is hot in there,' he said. 'Let's go into the conservatory.'

He stopped in the kitchen to pour two glasses of wine, while Nadine went on into the conservatory and sank down in one of Fee's cane chairs. The atmosphere was warm and moist and the air smelt of potting compost and the slightly heady scent from the many flowering plants which lined the shelves.

When Angelo joined her he handed her a glass of wine, before closing the door behind him and shutting out the noise of the party until it became merely a hum in the background.

He stood, looking down at her, his own glass cradled in one hand. He had discarded his jacket and undone the collar of his shirt. His tie lay loosely around his neck, a black band against the white shirt.

Briefly, when he had leaned forward to give her her drink, Nadine had caught a glimpse of the tangle of dark hair on his chest and was reminded of that moment in his room, when he had been wearing only his bathrobe, and of the emotions that had overwhelmed her then. The same turbulent emotions that had been threatening to get the better of her all evening.

She swallowed, searching desperately for something to say. 'You look very impressive tonight in evening dress,' she said at last.

'Ah,' he smiled glancing down at his shirt and trousers, 'I hired this, I must confess. I did not have anything like this with me. At home it is a different matter. . .all the time we go to the opera.'

'I hope you enjoyed this evening. . .I know it's very different from what you must be used to, but. . .' Nadine knew that she was beginning to waffle but the look in Angelo's eyes as he looked down at her was once again getting the better of her.

Ignoring what she was saying and leaning forward so that he was gazing directly into her eyes, he said softly, 'It does not bother you that your escort is paying more attention to your mother than to you?'

Nadine shook her head. 'No,' she said helplessly, 'not really.'

'Maybe you should be asking yourself why that is.'

'I think. . .' she took a deep breath, '. . .I think you may have a false impression of my relationship with Seymour,' she said at last.

'I think maybe I have,' he replied. 'In which case I think I would like you to enlighten me.'

'Seymour and I are friends,' she said, 'good friends.'

'And that is all?' The dark eyebrows rose enquiringly.

'Well. . .' she hesitated '. . .we are also colleagues, but you know that.'

'Yes,' he agreed, 'I know that. But this friendship. . . what does it involve?'

Nadine took a sip of her wine. Quite unexpectedly she thought that she had detected a note of jealousy in Angelo's voice, and suddenly she was beginning to enjoy herself. 'We both enjoy the theatre,' she began, 'and eating out—yes, we both enjoy eating out.' She paused, reflecting for a moment, then more seriously she said, 'Seymour was lonely after his wife died and I. . .' She trailed off, lost for words.

'And you, Nadine?' said Angelo softly. 'What about you?'

'What about me?' She looked up sharply.

'Are you lonely as well?'

'I suppose I get a bit lonely sometimes,' she admitted then quickly, before he had time to comment, she added, 'Oh, I have Paul, I know, and my mother and my friends at work, but. . .'

'Sometimes you need male company?' he asked softly.

'Yes, I suppose so.' She gave a helpless little shrug, not daring to meet his gaze again—afraid what she might see there.

'And romance?' He said it softly, so softly that she wondered for a moment if she had heard right.

'Romance? Oh, I don't know about that.' She gave a light laugh.

'Are you telling me there isn't any romance between you and Seymour?'

'Yes,' she said, then, 'I mean, no, there isn't. I don't think Seymour is into romance really. . .although, seeing him just now looking at my mother, I wonder if there is a side to him I haven't yet seen. . .!'

'And what of you, Nadine?' Gently Angelo touched her cheek just as he had done once before, and now— as then—her heart began to beat very fast. 'I thought. . .I thought you and Seymour. . .'

'No,' she said softly, 'no, really. There's nothing like that between Seymour and me.'

He was staring at her now with a kind of suppressed excitement in his eyes. 'Then surely there is nothing stopping us getting to know one another better? I ask you this before, Nadine, and you refuse me. I thought perhaps it was because of you and Seymour. Now you tell me there is nothing between you...so...?'

'But what of you?' she interrupted him quickly. 'What of your involvement?'

He frowned. 'I told you...thought I made it plain; I told both Karen and Lee I don't go out with them again—'

'Because you are committed elsewhere...' Nadine finished the sentence for him. 'That was the impression you gave, Angelo; that was the rumour that went round.'

'It was?' He raised his eyebrows.

'So, is it true?'

He stared at her for a long moment, then he laughed. 'Yes,' he sighed at last, 'yes, yes, it is true. I tell the others there is a lady. A lovely lady...'

'You shouldn't have led them on in the first place, Angelo,' she reproached him, at the same time thinking as he stood there before her, so casually handsome, that she couldn't blame anyone for falling for him.

'But I didn't know then,' he protested, and when he saw her frown he added, 'When I ask Lee to have a drink with me and Karen to play a game of squash, it was before I met my lovely lady. After I meet her...' he shrugged '...no one else matters...ever again.'

'But isn't she someone at home...in Italy...?' Even as she said it Nadine saw his expression change then he set his glass down and, moving towards her, took her hands in his.

'Nadine,' he said, and his voice was suddenly husky as he stared down at her, 'you are my lovely lady. You must know that. From the moment I saw you on that first morning I tell myself this is the lady I have been waiting for. All my life, I knew one day...and then there you were. Then you get angry with me—I think you don't like me. Then, when I think perhaps you do start to like me, I see you with Seymour and I think... Oh, I don't dare to tell you what I think. Now...now you tell me there is nothing with Seymour...so now there is no reason, no reason at all...'

She stared at him. As he had been speaking she had half known what was coming; had—from the look in his eyes...anticipated something of the sort.

But now that he'd said it she could hardly believe it. No reason, he'd said; no reason, she thought, except for the difference in their ages and...the fact that she had a teenage son.

Before she could voice any such fears Angelo spoke again.

'And you can't tell me that you don't want romance either,' he said, his voice breaking into her thoughts, 'because I just won't believe you.'

Releasing her, he took her face between both his hands and, tilting her chin upwards, compelled her to look into his eyes.

Nadine stared up at him, not knowing quite what to think. He was breathing heavily, while a pulse throbbed furiously at the side of his jaw. She knew that she was affected by him but she hadn't for one moment seriously considered that he might feel the same way about her.

His advances, his flattery, she had dismissed as being part of his charming, flirtatious nature—his behaviour towards her no more and no less than the way he behaved with all women.

Now he was telling her he wanted her.

Had he told all the others that as well? Lee, Karen—even Ruth?

She stared up at him and, quite suddenly, something told her that he hadn't.

'Nadine.' He was obviously struggling to get his emotions under some sort of control. 'Give me a chance, please?'

As she stared at him her mind was racing. Should she do as he said and give him a chance? It would never work, she knew that. There was too much against it and soon he would return to Italy, and that would surely be the end of any relationship.

But what of in the meantime. . .? What if she accepted it purely for what it was. . .? Accepted that it would end when he went home? Would it then be so terrible to have a fling with this exciting young man. . .?

There was silence around them, a silence so profound that Nadine fancied she heard, as well as saw, a geranium petal as it fell from the plant onto one of the slatted wooden shelves.

Even the distant buzz of the party seemed to have receded into obscurity, leaving herself and Angelo as alone as the sole survivors of some disaster.

'All right,' she heard someone say. 'Why not?'

It was only when she saw the joy that leapt into his eyes that she realised that it had been she who had spoken.

She was still in the same dream-like state when he took her hands again, drew her to her feet and kissed her—her cheeks, her eyelids, her forehead and finally her lips, parting them in that special way she remembered from the last time, the time she hadn't, try as she might, quite been able to forget.

And once again, in Angelo's arms and under his hands, she came alive. She forgot the party, the presence of Paul in the house, Fee and the fact that Seymour was still on the premises. Deeply buried desires had stirred on the last occasion Angelo had kissed her; this time they not only stirred they flared into reality and, as she wound her arms around his neck and responded to his kiss, her senses clamoured for more.

CHAPTER ELEVEN

'I'M UNDER no illusions.'

'Why not just enjoy it?'

'He's far too young for me.'

'Who says, for goodness' sake?'

It was a few days after the party, and Nadine was talking to Fee. Once again they were seated in the conservatory, but it was over breakfast on Nadine's day off; they were sharing a pot of coffee instead of a bottle of wine; the sun was shining, and this time Angelo was not there.

'He just is.' Nadine shrugged helplessly. 'I've never been into toyboys—you know that.'

'Angelo is hardly a toyboy,' said Fee firmly, pouring more coffee.

'Well, he's a good deal younger than me.'

'I can't see that it matters. You went out with Seymour, for heaven's sake, and he's old enough to be your father!'

'That's different—'

'I don't see why—'

'It wasn't that sort of relationship—Seymour always knew that, and so did I. Speaking of which. . .' Nadine raised a speculative eyebrow in her mother's direction '. . .you seemed to be getting on rather well with Seymour the other night; either that, or my eyes were deceiving me.'

'Seymour's a charming man,' replied Fee, apparently unperturbed by Nadine's slightly accusing tone. 'But it's Angelo we are talking about, not Seymour. What exactly is the age difference between you two?'

'I'm not sure,' admitted Nadine, 'and, I have to con-

fess, I'm afraid to ask. But he can only be around his
mid to late twenties.'

'So what if he is? What are ten years?' Fee shrugged,
then she frowned. 'Is it Paul you're worried about?
Because if it is,' she went on, not giving Nadine a chance
to answer, 'don't be. Paul thinks Angelo is terrific. He
told me so, and it's not just because of his motorbike,
either.'

'Maybe,' said Nadine drily, 'but it might be a different
matter now that I'm actually having a relationship
with him.'

'So you are, then?' Fee chuckled and sipped her
coffee.

'What?'

'Having a relationship with him.'

Nadine sighed. 'Yes, I am.'

'You didn't like him at first, did you?' Fee was suddenly curious.

'No, I didn't,' Nadine replied frankly. 'I thought he
was simply a conceited flirt who thought he was God's
gift to women.'

'And now?' asked Fee.

'What do you mean, ''now''?' Nadine looked up
sharply.

'What do you think of him now? What's happened
in such a relatively short space of time to make you
change your opinion to such an extent that you are
having a relationship with him?'

'I'm not sure, really.' Nadine frowned, helplessly
watching a trickle of condensation as it meandered down
a pane of glass on the door of the conservatory. 'I guess
I saw another side of him,' she admitted at last.

'At work?' asked Fee.

She nodded, 'Yes, partly at work. I saw,' she went on,
after a moment's reflection, 'instead of a self-obsessed
egotist, I saw a caring, dedicated man—a man who put
people's well-being before himself, before his career. I
liked that.'

'And out of work? What have you seen there?'

'A different man. A man who makes me feel like a woman again.'

'You're in love with him,' said Fee candidly.

'I don't know.' Nadine's reply was swift, sharp. 'It's too soon to say. Besides, I don't want that to happen. It won't come to anything.'

'You're afraid of being hurt again,' said Fee.

'Maybe I am.'

'You've never really loved anyone since Julian, have you?'

'There have been others. . . .well, one or two,' Nadine began, 'but. . .' She shrugged and trailed off, leaving the sentence unfinished. It was true that there had been a couple of others but what her mother had just said was also true—she had never really loved anyone since Julian; had never trusted herself to fall in love again after being so badly hurt.

'I still think you should just enjoy this.' Fee stood up and began to put the blue and white breakfast china onto a tray. 'Take it as it comes. See what happens. Honestly, love. You are still a young woman, a lovely young woman. It is my dearest wish to see you happy again one day and I know your father felt the same way.'

Nadine felt her eyes mist over at mention of her father, and in a deliberate attempt to lighten the mood she got swiftly to her feet. 'You talk as if I never have any fun. But I do. . . Paul and I still have fun together.'

'Paul won't be here for ever,' said Fee gently. 'There'll be university in a couple of years. He has his own life to lead.'

'I know,' said Nadine, following Fee into the house. 'You don't need to remind me.'

Life for Nadine seemed to take on a magical quality over the next few weeks. At first she and Angelo simply spent time together, getting to know each other. He took her out—to restaurants where they would spend hours over a single meal, talking and telling each other of their lives before the moment they had met, or they would take the Harley and ride for miles deep into the heart of the English countryside, stopping at a pub for lunch or a drink.

Occasionally, if they went by car, Paul and Fee would go with them. Or sometimes they would all watch Paul play football for his school, ending up—more often than not—in Fee's kitchen, where Angelo would cook Italian pasta for supper.

On the ward there were a few raised eyebrows amongst the staff at Nadine's and Angelo's liaison. Lee Bevan was heard to comment that she wished she'd known when Nadine had warned her about Angelo that she'd wanted the registrar for herself, but it all proved to be a nine-day wonder and everyone eventually got used to it—even Karen Ashton, who at first had continued to be openly hostile to them both, in the end gave up and accepted it.

Amongst the patients, Barry Fletcher openly expressed his pleasure before he went home to continue his convalescence, while Jennifer Dickinson—who learnt of the situation just before she was discharged—was openly envious. 'Good for you,' she said to Nadine. 'I wish it were me. Since my divorce I just don't seem to be able to get any relationship right—there always seems to be a snag.'

'There could be with this,' said Nadine wryly, 'namely the fact that he's younger than me.'

'That's not a snag,' replied Jennifer crisply, 'that's a bonus.'

Nadine still wasn't convinced—even when shortly after she and Angelo had started going out together the talk one night turned to birth signs and she learned that he had been born under the star sign of Gemini and, during the same conversation, she discovered to her surprise that he was, in fact, twenty nine.

'I thought you were younger than that,' she admitted.

'I know you did,' he laughed teasingly. 'I've always looked younger than I am. I'm not sure whether it's an advantage or not.'

'Well, I'm glad you aren't quite as young as I thought.'

'I told you. It makes no difference. No difference at all,' he replied.

He also told her again that there wasn't anyone else in his life—no one at home in Italy, as she had once suspected there might have been.

'I once promised my mother,' he said on another occasion, 'that I will marry when I am thirty—provided, of course, I've met the right woman.'

Nadine, remembering what Seymour had told her about the Fabrielli family and the continuation of the bloodline, remained silent.

The chill, blustery days of spring gave way to soft rain and bright sunshine, and Angelo's time at the Spencer Rathbone began to run out. Bob Jenkins recovered sufficiently from his injuries to be able to return home but Josh Barnes, beset by new complications, remained.

'I've seen so many come and go since I've been here,' Josh told Nadine one morning. 'I've got a job to remember them all now.'

'Never mind, Josh,' she said. 'You're improving all the time.'

'Am I?' he said, a hopeless note in his voice. 'I sometimes wonder.'

'Mr Russell is very pleased with you. He said as much only this morning.'

Josh visibly brightened then, changing the subject, said, 'Dr Fabrielli is going back to Italy soon, isn't he?'

'Yes, he is.' Nadine's reply was spontaneous but deep inside she felt a pang.

'Why can't he stay?' asked Josh.

'He was only here for a short time because his Italian boss wanted him to work alongside Mr Russell to gain experience.'

'You'll miss him, won't you?' asked Josh with all the candour and innocence of the young.

'Yes, Josh,' Nadine, who would once have exercised wariness at confirming such a statement, found herself agreeing. 'I will miss him.' What was the point of denying it when everyone knew anyway?

Even Ruth Stannard had conquered her jealousy and once, briefly, allowed her bland mask to slip. 'I wouldn't let him go if I were you,' she said to Nadine, adding caustically, 'You won't get another opportunity like this.'

'No, Ruth,' Nadine sighed, ignoring the barb, 'I don't suppose I shall.'

By then, of course, she knew that she was in love with him; had known for some time but their agreement had been to enjoy the moment, each day as it came, with no talk of the future.

That he would soon return to Italy and his old way of life, she knew only too well. He had to go, she knew that also; there was no question of his staying and there never had been. His position in Orthopaedics, as she had explained to Josh, had been purely temporary.

Was her place in his heart temporary as well? When he got back to his work, his family and his friends, would he forget her?

Probably, in spite of her caution, she was about to be hurt again. For that reason she had avoided the deepening of their relationship, but when the inevitability of it became a foregone conclusion she abandoned caution on the assumption that if she was going to be hurt she might as well have as much to remember as possible.

As spring gave way to summer they made love for the first time—deep in a woodland glade surrounded by a sea of bluebells, the silence broken only by the sweet, penetrating song of a blackbird and then by Angelo at the height of their passion as he called her name.

Only a short while before, as they had walked across the fields to the woods, Angelo had asked her to marry him and then had stifled any response she might have been about to make with a kiss.

'Don't answer right away,' he'd said. 'I want you to be sure.'

Now, in the aftermath of their love, they lay together, with the vast summer sky above them and the warm mossy earth beneath, at perfect peace—Angelo with his head cradled on her breasts, his dark hair in stark contrast to the whiteness of her skin.

'I love you, Sister Hadley.' Gently he teased one nipple with his tongue.

'I love you too, Dr Fabrielli.' Nadine arched her back slightly as a sweet shaft of desire shot through her again.

He must have felt the spasm because he looked up and gave his lazy smile before he began to caress her again, his hands moving expertly over her body— arousing and demanding.

'You can't be ready again,' she protested, 'not so soon.'

'Really?' He moved, proving without any doubt that he was. 'You have some complaint?'

'Oh, no, Doctor.' She sighed, stretching out beneath him once more. 'No complaints at all.'

And later, satiated by the intensity of their passion, they lay safe in the cocoon of each other's arms and Angelo said, 'I know I said take your time with your reply, but you won't take too long, will you?' Raising himself on one elbow, he gazed anxiously down at her.

'Angelo. . .' she took a deep breath '. . .before I give you my answer there's something you need to know.'

His eyes narrowed slightly but he said, 'Whatever it is, it won't make any difference to the way I feel.'

'Maybe not,' she replied, 'But you need to know, anyway. You see, when Paul was born I was very ill—in fact, I nearly died. I was told afterwards that I probably wouldn't be able to have more children.'

As she finished speaking Nadine scanned his face. Briefly she saw some emotion enter his dark eyes and then it was gone, so quickly that she wondered if she might have imagined it.

'It makes no difference,' he said. 'It is you I love, and if it is not meant for us to have children then so be it. Paul is your son. He may not want me to be a father to him, but we will be friends—that much I know.'

'But you—what about you, Angelo? You will want children of your own one day.'

'I want you, Nadine. If, by some miracle, you are able to give me a child that would be wonderful... If not,' he shrugged, 'it will not be the end of the world. We will be happy.'

'And what of your family?' she asked anxiously.

'They will be happy too,' he said firmly. 'They will love you, Nadine. You will see.' Bending his head, he kissed the tip of her nose. 'So how long will you make me wait? I have to go back to Rome very soon... Will you tell me before I go?'

'Oh, Angelo,' she whispered, 'I won't make you wait. I love you so much and, yes, of course I will marry you.'

His shout of joy echoed through the glade, startling the birds—who rose from the trees, squawking and flapping with indignation.

'I want you to come out to Rome,' he said as they strolled back through the field to the lay-by where he had parked the Harley.

'To Rome?' She paused.

'Yes, I want you to meet my family and we need to talk about our future and where we will live and work.'

So caught up in her own joy and happiness had Nadine become that she hadn't really stopped to think of the practicalities of the future.

Angelo's work was in Rome. Hers was in England. One of them would have to give up their job. Then there was Paul, who was at a crucial stage in his schooling... And Fee... The difficulties would be endless.

'We will get round them,' he said when she voiced her fears. 'We will take things one step at a time. First we must tell Paul and Fee, then you must see if you can take some time off to join me in Rome for a few days.'

Fee, predictably, was delighted when they broke the news to her. Paul, too, seemed pleased but later, when they were alone, Nadine questioned him more closely.

'Of course I'm pleased, Mum,' he said. 'Angelo's a great guy. I'm just glad you'll have someone to keep an eye on you. I won't always be around, you know.'

'I know,' she replied seriously.

'Besides,' Paul went on, 'Angelo's told me he will get tickets for me to go to Rome for the European Cup Match—Scotty will be dead jealous. You know. . .' he paused, '. . .I quite like the idea of having an Italian stepfather—it's certainly different. Loads of guys at school have stepfathers, but none are Italians.'

'There can't be too many who ride Harley Davidsons, either,' remarked Nadine drily. She was so relieved that Paul was happy with the situation. The love that she and Angelo had for each other could so easily have been marred if Paul had disliked him.

Angelo told Seymour Russell the news and when the consultant spoke to Nadine, wishing her happiness, she thought for one moment that she detected a hint of sadness in his eyes.

'Angelo's a lucky man,' he said. 'I wish I were twenty years younger.'

'I know the feeling,' said Nadine wryly. 'I look at Angelo sometimes and wish I, too, were younger. Ten years younger at least.'

'Rubbish,' said Seymour. 'You two have a lifetime ahead of you. By the way,' he said, 'I've told Angelo there will always be a place on my team for him here at the Rathbone if he wants it.'

'That's kind of you, Seymour.'

'Not really,' he replied. 'It's just wishful thinking. Young Fabrielli's a damn fine surgeon. The world will be his oyster—I can see him having his pick of all the top hospitals.'

The ward staff became caught up in the romance and excitement of the situation.

'Oh, I wish it were me,' said Lee with a sigh. 'I've always wanted to go to Italy—and with Angelo Fabrielli as well!'

'You should think yourself lucky you've ended up with Dean Gardiner,' Ruth snapped acidly.

'Well, yes, I do,' said Lee, 'but even so. . .'

'I'm so pleased for you, Nadine.' Jayne hugged her tightly when she heard the news. 'But does this mean we are going to lose you completely?'

'Nothing's been decided yet,' said Nadine. 'That's what these few days in Rome are all about.'

On the night before Angelo's departure Nadine clung to him in a sudden wave of desolation, as if somehow with his going the spell would be broken.

'It isn't for long.' Tenderly he held her. 'Soon we will be together again.'

'But even then it will only be for a short time. I will have to return, Angelo.'

'I know. But soon you will be my wife, then nothing will part us ever again.'

After his departure the longing for him became so great that Nadine found herself counting not only the days but the hours and minutes until they could be together again.

Three weeks later, early one morning when the hazy mist held a promise of the heat to come, he was at Rome airport to meet her.

She had worried on the flight that something might have changed; that Angelo would be different in some way; that he might have realised that his feelings for her had changed. But as soon as she saw him—the same dear Angelo, the handsome face, the dark eyes anxiously scanning the faces of the disembarking passengers—her heart leapt with an overwhelming surge of love for him.

And moments later, when she felt his arms around her and his lips on hers, her fears were allayed because she knew that nothing had changed.

'I've missed you, Sister Hadley,' he murmured against her hair. 'Have you missed me?'

'Just a bit, Dr Fabrielli, just a bit,' she replied.

He drove her straight to his apartment—this time not on a motorbike but in a black Ferrari—an old building in a secluded, sun-dappled piazza in the very heart of the ancient city.

She saw little of the sights of Rome on the drive; took in very little of her surroundings as they took the lift to the top floor of the apartment. Her only concern was that they were together once more.

They had barely got inside the room before Angelo kicked the door shut behind them and drew her into his arms, and so desperate was their haste to love each other—to possess each other again—that within minutes their clothes formed a frantic trail into the bedroom.

It wasn't until later that Nadine was to appreciate her surroundings—the shuttered rooms, the polished wooden floors, the old dark furniture, the flowers and the freshly scented crisp cotton bedlinen.

This time there was no holding back, no restraint, and as Angelo tore off his shirt Nadine sank down across his bed. Her welcome was absolute, with no trace of hesitation, as desperately they sought satisfaction from the frustrations of being apart. Their release was sweet, but piercing and intense, and afterwards they lay in each other's arms, only superficially fulfilled.

Later Angelo disappeared to the kitchen of his apartment, returning with a simple meal of fruit, cheese, bread and wine. They talked during their meal, bringing each other up to date with all that had happened in their separate worlds in the short time they had been apart, and afterwards they made love again. But this time in a more leisurely fashion, the edge having been taken from their desperate need of each other.

This time they indulged in a long, slow arousing of the senses, culminating in a release just as sweet, but deeper and infinitely more satisfying for them both.

Afterwards they slept in each other's arms, a sleep of peace and contentment.

CHAPTER TWELVE

FOR three days Nadine and Angelo lived for each other, with most of the first day being spent in bed.

Then very gradually they began to emerge from the apartment—first for food, then to sit in the sunshine in the piazza and later for a sightseeing tour of the city.

Nadine was captivated and fell under the spell of the Eternal City from the very start, marvelling at its wonders and at how much of the ancient city remained alongside the modern—amazed at the thousands of tourists and pilgrims who thronged St Peter's Square and sharing with them the splendour of the Vatican and the Sistine Chapel.

They dined in small, intimate restaurants and, on their third night, he took her to the Trevi fountain, where he insisted that she threw her coins into the water.

'To ensure your return to Rome,' he told her seriously, then he drove high onto one of the seven hills that surrounded the city to show her the view by night.

'It's wonderful,' she sighed, leaning against him, 'quite wonderful.'

'Tomorrow,' he said softly, enfolding her in his arms, 'I take you to meet my family.'

'Angelo?' she asked later when they were in bed, 'you have told them about me, haven't you? Your family, I mean.'

'Of course,' he said. 'Of course I tell them. They all look forward to meeting you.'

But the next morning, when Nadine awoke—long before Angelo—she wondered with some anxiety exactly what he had told them.

Turning her head, she watched him as he slept.

He looked so young and so vulnerable in sleep—the dark hair tousled, the black lashes thick against his cheek.

Her heart flooded with love for him, but her love was still tinged with fear—the fear that any woman had who was to marry a younger man. The fear that one day, when her looks had faded and he was in his prime, he might be attracted to a younger, lovelier woman.

Sunlight was seeping through the slats in the wooden shutters and outside she could hear the early morning activities as the piazza came alive. Suddenly she wished that they could stay here today and not go to see Angelo's family.

She wanted to keep him to herself and not share him with anyone; to spend her last day in Rome in the same way as they had spent the others, just being alone together.

But she couldn't be that selfish, she knew that. His family meant as much to him as Paul and Fee did to her, and he quite obviously was looking forward to taking her to meet them.

During their time in Rome they still hadn't discussed their future and where they would live after they were married. It was almost as if both of them had deliberately avoided the issue, delaying the decision until the last possible moment.

The previous morning Angelo had taken her to the huge modern hospital in Rome where he worked. She had met the world-renowned surgeon, Giovanni Ligorio, who headed the orthopeadic team and she could not have failed to notice how delighted he seemed at Angelo's return.

Deep down she knew that she should make it easy for Angelo and say that she was prepared to join him in Rome after they were married.

If only Paul was already at university. . . If only. . .

'What are you thinking?' His voice broke into her

thoughts and, turning her head, Nadine saw that he had awoken, and was watching her.

'I was thinking about us,' she said. 'About the future.'

'Ah,' he said softly, 'the future.' Turning to her, he began caressing her shoulder lazily. 'I think,' he went on, 'the future stretches for a long time. I think the future may take care of itself. At the moment I am more concerned about the present.'

With a sigh she turned towards him and, dismissing the complications that the future might present, gave herself up to the sheer bliss of being loved by him once more.

They travelled in the Ferrari for about thirty kilometres to the Tivoli region on the very outskirts of Rome.

The Villa Fabrielli, surrounded by tall poplars and cypress trees, was hidden from the road behind a high stone wall. As they passed through wrought-iron gates Angelo pointed to plaques set at frequent intervals in the railings.

'Look,' he said, 'each one bears the family crest and the initial F.'

Afterwards Nadine decided that it was then that she had felt the first twinge of unease, but for the moment she could only gape at the splendour of her surroundings.

The formal gardens on either side of the long sweeping drive were edged with tall, dark conifers, affording the occasional glimpse of marble statues, sparkling fountains or secret arbours, but it was the house itself at the very top of the drive that really took her breath away.

It was a long, low building of ancient grey stone beneath a roof of ridged tiles, with a central tower and graceful arched windows.

As Angelo brought the Ferrari to a halt with a crunching of gravel a manservant appeared at the entrance and greeted him in obvious delight.

Angelo, smiling, returned the greeting, helped Nadine from the car, took her hand and led her into the house.

She was vaguely aware of a vast, mosaic-tiled hallway and plastered walls with painted murals, of stairs that soared high into the tower, of the voices of Angelo and the manservant—echoing as if in a void—then of marble pillars and a series of archways which led from one sumptuously furnished room to another until eventually they stepped out onto a sun-dappled terrace, with a view of what seemed like the whole of Italy spread before them.

And it was there, beneath a vine-covered loggia, that the entire Fabrielli family were congregated, waiting to greet them.

In a daze Nadine was introduced to Angelo's father, then his mother, his grandmother, an aunt, his two sisters and their husbands and children. Then, the pleasantries over, they took their places around a huge central table for an open-air lunch.

By then her earlier feelings of unease had grown to such proportions that they had settled like a pall of foreboding as she struggled to eat.

Angelo's family spoke very little English, with the exception of one of his sisters—Maria—whose command of the language was almost as fluent as his own, so communication was difficult and only gradually did Nadine begin to recover from the shock she had experienced. She had expected wealth, but nothing like this, and when she finally recovered sufficiently to take further stock of her surroundings she became aware that she was the object of much scrutiny.

Angelo's mother, especially, hardly seemed to take her eyes off her and, to her dismay, Nadine realised that this elegant, exquisitely groomed woman could not have been much more than ten years older than herself and that the look in her eyes, as she, too, recognised that same fact, was one of disappointment.

His father was older—a cultured, shrewd-looking man, short and balding but with his son's smile and infinite charm.

After the meal Nadine, to her relief, was borne away by Maria to view the fountains in the water-gardens below the terrace.

'This is your first visit to Rome?' Maria asked as they began to descend a steep flight of stone steps at one corner of the terrace.

'Yes, it is.' With a backward glance at Angelo, who smiled encouragingly at her before he strolled into the villa with his mother who had linked her arm in his, Nadine added, 'It is a magnificent city.'

'So, how long have you known my brother?' The question appeared casual but the glance that Maria threw her was speculative.

'Nearly three months,' replied Nadine steadily, determined not to be intimidated.

'So little time and yet already you know you wish to marry him?' Maria spoke lightly, but in that moment Nadine recognised that Maria, doubtless for her linguistic skills, had been the one delegated by the rest of the family to do the necessary interrogations.

'I love Angelo very much,' she said simply.

'As I am sure he loves you.' Maria inclined her head.

They continued to descend the steps in silence, then Maria said, 'This must be very daunting for you—meeting us all like this. The Fabrielli family *en masse* can appear quite formidable, I am sure.'

'Not at all,' murmured Nadine, 'although I must admit I was surprised. . .' She stopped and looked back. 'The house and everything—I never expected anything like it. . .'

'Angelo did not tell you about his home. . .about the Villa Fabrielli?' There was surprise in Maria's voice.

'Well, yes, I suppose he did.' Nadine paused, then realised that Maria was waiting for her to continue. 'He certainly didn't try to hide anything,' she went on at last, 'but so often the reality of something is very different from what one has imagined.'

Maria laughed and tossed back her long black hair,

revealing expensive gold hoops in her ears. 'My mother
will be pleased he is to marry at last,' she went on as
they reached the foot of the steps. 'I think she was
beginning to despair. Angelo is the rebel of the family,
you see. Already he has displeased my father by not
going into the family business. It was also beginning to
look as if he wasn't going to present them with the
much-needed heir to carry on the family name. . .' She
flashed Nadine another look. 'I understand you already
have a son?' she said unexpectedly.

'Yes, yes, I have,' answered Nadine. 'Paul is sixteen.'

'Really?' Maria sounded surprised, and Nadine wondered if Angelo had deliberately withheld that particular
piece of information from his family.

'You have children, don't you?' she said hurriedly.
'Two of those little ones were yours, weren't they?'
They had stopped before a fountain whose jets of water
cascaded noisily into a deep pool of turquoise. Around
them the scent of jasmine from the many shrubs that
edged the pathways hung heavily in the air.

'Three of them, actually.' Maria laughed. 'The other
two are my sister's children.'

'So your parents already have five grandchildren?'

'Yes, they do,' agreed Maria, and after a long pause
she said, 'But none of the children are Fabriellis. My
father and my grandmother are quite desperate for a
Fabrielli heir—that is why they all stare at you at lunch.
Oh, they did,' she cried when Nadine would have protested, 'of course they did. It is down to Angelo to
continue the bloodline. . .and to you now. . .'

'But what of your brother?' Nadine heard herself say
in sudden desperation. 'Angelo told me you have a
brother. Isn't he married; doesn't he have children?'

Maria turned to her in amazement. 'Yes, yes,' she
said, 'we do have a brother, but didn't Angelo tell you?'

'Tell me what?' Nadine stared at her as the water
continued to crash and foam behind them.

'Our brother, Raphael, is still a student. . .'

'But later. . .surely. . .?'

'He is in the seminary in Rome,' Maria said, and there was no disguising the pride in her voice. 'Raphael is training for the priesthood.'

The rest of the day passed in a blur for Nadine, as if she was witnessing events through a rather inefficient telescope. The family continued to be courteous, polite and charming but it was with a decided sense of relief that she took her place beside Angelo in the Ferrari at the end of the visit and waved goodbye to the family as they stood outside the Villa Fabrielli.

They spent their last evening in the little restaurant that had become their favourite, before returning to Angelo's apartment.

'I don't think I was what your family expected,' Nadine said at last, voicing her unease which had been mounting all day.

'What do you mean?' Angelo's reply was light-hearted, teasing, but with an underlying hint of anxiety as if he had picked up on her fears but didn't want to admit to them.

'I think perhaps they were disappointed,' she replied quietly.

'This is nonsense,' he said quickly—too quickly, she thought. 'They love you, as I knew they would, as I love you, Nadine.'

She said no more but later, in the deep of the night, after they had made love he held her close and said, 'I don't want you to go.'

'I love you, Angelo,' she whispered, clinging to him in a kind of desperation.

'Come back to me soon,' he said, 'then we can be married.'

She knew then what he hadn't seemed quite able to tell her—that he expected her to return home, give in her notice at the Spencer Rathbone and return to him so that they could be married as quickly as possible.

'I will start to look for a home for us,' he said just before they parted at the airport the following morning, and although he told her over and over again that he loved her Nadine's heart was heavy as her plane took off. By the time she reached Heathrow she knew, without a shadow of doubt, what it was she had to do.

She wrote the letter as soon as she arrived home, telling him that in spite of the fact she loved him more than she had ever loved anyone before—or, perhaps, because of it—she couldn't marry him.

You had almost convinced me that the difference in our ages didn't matter. You had also almost convinced me that the fact I might not be able to give you a child didn't matter. But seeing your family and hearing their hopes and dreams brought it home to me that, while it might not matter to you now, in the future it could matter a great deal—so much so that it could destroy our relationship.

On a purely selfish note, she went on,

I also realised whilst I was in Rome that, although I would be quite happy to live anywhere in the world with you eventually, at the present time I cannot leave England—at least not until Paul's future is settled. I couldn't expect you to disrupt your career for me and I wouldn't ask you to.

I love you, my darling Angelo. You brought so much love and laughter into my life and restored something within me that I thought had died for ever. I hope one day you find the kind of happiness you deserve.

She told only Fee what had happened, simply explaining the facts and giving her reasons for ending the relationship. When she had finished and her mother remained silent she threw her a sharp glance.

'You don't understand, do you?' she said.

Fee gave a deep sigh and stood up. They were sitting in the garden at Montague House, the conservatory doors flung wide behind them as—surrounded by the scent of roses and freshly cut grass—they watched Paul mow the lawn. 'I understand your reasons only too well,' she said, 'but I happen to think you're wrong. I happen to think that if you love each other, which you two quite obviously do, then all other obstacles should not be insurmountable.'

'You always were an incurable romantic,' said Nadine drily, looking up at Fee. 'Well, I can't take that chance. I don't want another relationship going sour on me—which I think there is every danger that this one might after a few years.'

'I'm sure you are exaggerating,' said Fee, leaning across the crazy-paving pathway to pick a fully blown rose.

'You didn't see his family,' muttered Nadine.

'I can't believe they were really that bad.' Her mother sniffed deeply at the rose, burying her face in the soft pink petals.

'Well, if you can imagine the Mafia, the Royal Family and the cast of *Dallas* all rolled into one you would have a pretty good idea of the Fabrielli family...'

'Oh, come on!' Fee looked incredulous, but at the same time amused, at Nadine's description.

'Well, perhaps they weren't that bad,' said Nadine with a sniff. 'If I'm honest,' she went on, after a moment's reflection, 'they were charming, and the villa—well, it was out of this world! But I think that was the problem... Honestly, Mum, they aren't a bit like us; they—'

'There can't be a lot wrong with them to have produced someone like Angelo,' protested Fee. 'Honestly, Nadine, think about it. There is a young man who has everything that money can buy, by the sounds of it, but

what does he choose to do? Squander it all? Live like
a playboy? No, he chooses to be a surgeon!'

'I'm not saying there was anything wrong with them,'
muttered Nadine with a quick, dismissive gesture. 'Just
different. Very, very different,' she added.

'What about his mother?' Fee turned curiously to
look at her.

'It was his mother who bothered me the most,' Nadine
replied shrewdly. 'And that was probably because I'm
a mother myself and I know how I would respond in
the same situation if it was Paul.' As she spoke she
narrowed her eyes and stared down the garden at her
son, who at that moment glanced up as if he knew he
was being discussed. He could not have heard them
above the sound of the mower, but he waved.

'So, what did she say?' Fee sat down again on the
garden bench beside Nadine.

'It wasn't so much what she said,' reflected Nadine.
'In fact, she spoke very little English.'

'So, what, then?' Fee persisted.

'It was the look in her eyes when she first saw me
and she realised I was older than Angelo.'

'Hadn't he told her that?' Fee frowned. 'Didn't she
know about Paul?'

'Oh, yes, he'd told his family that I had a son.' Nadine
paused, watching Paul again. 'I think he'd just omitted
to tell them how old he is—or how old I am, for that
matter,' she added bitterly after a moment.

'Nadine. . .' Fee took a deep breath '. . .I keep telling
you the age difference between you and Angelo is
nothing. . .'

'Maybe not. . .' Nadine shrugged '. . .but the possibility of my not being able to give Angelo a child is another
matter altogether.'

'But you have Paul. . . Angelo is very fond of Paul. . .
Or maybe, on the other hand, you could adopt. . .'

'Mother, for goodness' sake!' Nadine turned to Fee in
sudden exasperation. 'I'm far too old to adopt. Besides,

adoption wouldn't come into it. The Fabriellis want a
male heir to carry on the name. . .the line. . .the family
business. . .I don't know.' She threw up her hands in
despair. 'Whatever it is, I can't give it to them.'

'I thought you said they have grandchildren already?'
Fee frowned, a stubborn expression settling onto
her face.

'They do,' said Nadine wearily.

'Well, then. . .'

'They are his sisters' children,' she explained
patiently. 'Not Fabriellis which, to that family, is not
the same thing at all.'

'They should count their blessings,' muttered Fee
darkly, then looked up quickly as if she had suddenly
remembered something and said, 'Didn't Angelo say he
had a brother?'

'He did.'

'So?'

'No, Mother.' Nadine stood up. 'Catholic priests
aren't allowed to have children, even if their name does
happen to be Fabrielli. Now, if you don't mind,' she
said firmly, 'I would like the matter closed. I don't want
to discuss it any more.'

'What have you told Paul?' In the sudden silence Fee
miserably looked down the garden towards her grand-
son, who had just switched off the mower.

'Simply that things didn't work out, that's all,' replied
Nadine.

'How did he take it?'

'He's been very quiet. But he'll get over it. Far better
now than later. . .' she trailed off then, putting her head
down to hide the tears that had suddenly filled her eyes,
she hurried into the house.

When Nadine returned to work she told only Jayne what
had happened, and even then she gave just the barest
details. 'Maybe you could put the others in the picture,'

she concluded. 'You see, I don't want to talk about it, Jayne.'

'Of course, Nadine. . .but I'm sorry,' said Jayne. 'Oh, I'm so very sorry.'

'Don't worry,' Nadine replied briskly. 'I'll survive. . . no doubt.'

And survive she did, putting on such a brave face to the outside world that no one suspected that inside she was dying. That when she was alone at night she cried desperate tears, while her body ached and yearned for Angelo and her mind played dangerous tricks so that she imagined herself back in Rome—in a sun-drenched piazza with marble statues and cool fountains, on a hill high above the Eternal City or dining alfresco beneath a vine-covered loggia as an accepted, beloved part of Angelo's family.

She threw herself into her work, always having been a firm believer that hard work was the only antidote for any broken relationship.

Patients continued to come and go on Orthopaedics, the only one remaining from Angelo's time being Josh Barnes—and even he was hopeful of an imminent return home.

'You've done a marvellous job with Josh,' she told Seymour one morning as together they studied the boy's X-rays. 'You've virtually repaired a shattered body.'

'I have to confess the boy has been a challenge,' said Seymour, squinting critically at the plates. 'The right femur, I fear, will always be weak and he will require many months of intensive physiotherapy, but I'm confident he will win through in the end. The boy has great determination.'

'Did you see Bob Jenkins last week?' asked Nadine, her gaze suddenly falling on Bob's records.

'Yes,' Seymour replied, 'he came to Outpatients for his follow-up appointment. He, too, has made an excellent recovery.'

'And Barry Fletcher? Has he had his follow-up yet?'

'No, that's next week, I believe.' Seymour paused. 'I did see Jennifer Dickinson, though,' he added.

'And how was she?' asked Nadine quickly.

'Not good.' Seymour shook his head. 'She's back on dihyrocodeine. I'm going to see her again in a month but I fear a spinal fusion may be necessary in her case. She is still in a great deal of pain. I had hoped the laminectomy would have been sufficient but. . .' he shrugged '. . .that's the way it goes.'

'Poor Jennifer,' said Nadine. 'A victim of her occupation, I fear.'

Seymour nodded and turned as if to leave the office then he stopped and hesitated, glancing at Nadine as if he wanted to say something but didn't know quite how. He hadn't mentioned Angelo since her return and she didn't know whether Jayne had put him in the picture or not. In the end he looked so uncomfortable that she decided to put him out of his misery.

'When I was in Rome,' she began, and his head shot up, 'I went to the hospital where I met Giovanni Ligorio.'

'He's one of the finest surgeons in the world. . .' Seymour mused.

'He sang your praises as well,' remarked Nadine.

'I. . .er. . .I take it young Fabrielli has returned to work with him?'

'I would imagine so. . .'

Seymour cleared his throat. 'I'm sorry,' he said, 'about what happened. . .' He was clearly embarrassed and, hoping once more to put him at ease, Nadine quickly asked,

'Jayne told you. . .?'

'Jayne?' He threw her another glance. 'No,' he said, 'no, not Jayne. . .'

'Then who?' she frowned.

'It was Fee, actually.' Noisily he cleared his throat again.

'Fee?' Nadine stared at him.

'Yes, we...er...we went to a matinée the other after-noon, then had tea together...I ... er...you're not upset, are you...?'

'Upset?' She continued to stare at him. 'Why ever should I be upset?'

'I don't know,' he said helplessly. 'Fee thought you might be. You see, Nadine, it was when you were in Rome. Fee was going to tell you herself when you came back but then when you did and told her about you and young Fabrielli—about it being off and all that—she couldn't bring herself to tell you...thought you might be upset...'

'Oh, Seymour...' she stared at him '...how could I be upset?'

'Well, you see...' he looked even more embarrassed, '...I must confess I'm getting quite fond of your mother...and...'

'Seymour, I'm delighted!' she exclaimed. 'Honestly, I am,' she went on when he looked far from convinced. 'How could I be otherwise? Two of the people I love the most, finding happiness in each other's company— my mother and my dearest friend—how could I be upset?'

As his face began to clear she stood on tiptoe and, reaching up, kissed him lightly on the cheek.

'I wish it could have worked out for you,' he mumbled.

'Think nothing of it,' she said brightly. 'I'll get over it.' But as she watched him walk away down the corridor she had to battle to get rid of the lump in her throat.

'You're a dark horse,' she said later to her mother. 'Why didn't you tell me about you and Seymour?'

'Oh, darling, how could I after what had happened? Oh, I was so looking forward to telling you at first, but when you came back you looked so...I don't know, so lost I simply didn't have the heart. And I wasn't quite sure how you'd take it, anyway.'

'Why?'

'Well, Seymour was your friend. . .'

'What do you mean, "was"?' Nadine retorted. "I hope he still is.'

'Well, yes,' Fee replied hastily. 'Yes, of course he is. . . But you know what I mean.'

'Yes, Mum,' Nadine sighed. 'Yes, I know what you mean. But you mustn't worry about it. Seymour is a friend, a very dear friend, but it was never more than that. He knows it, and so do I.'

'Nadine?' Fee hesitated. 'Have you heard from Angelo since your return?'

'No.' She shook her head. 'Neither do I expect to. I dare say when he got my letter he was relieved he'd been let off so lightly once he'd got used to the idea. I'm sure for him it must have been like one of those holiday romances that fade as quickly as a suntan on returning home.'

'Oh, Nadine, I'm sure it wasn't like that.' Fee looked troubled. 'I'm sure he's suffering every bit as much as you.'

'Who says I'm suffering, for heaven's sake?'

'I do,' replied Fee crisply.

'I can assure you—' Nadine began, but she was cut short.

'You may be able to fool all the others,' said Fee, 'but you can't fool me. I'm your mother.'

During the second week after Nadine's return from Rome there was a serious road traffic accident in Hawksford. A motorbike was in collision with an articulated lorry, which jackknifed and careered into a minibus.

The lorry driver and two of the elderly passengers in the minibus were killed instantly and the survivors, including the motorcyclist, were brought into the accident and emergency department of the Spencer Rathbone.

Most of the injured required orthopaedic surgery. Nadine's ward was packed to overflowing and as the bed situation became desperate routine operations scheduled for the following day had to be cancelled.

'This is ridiculous!' snapped Ruth, as she and Nadine waited at the lift to receive yet another patient. 'We can't be expected to cope.'

'Oh, but we are,' replied Nadine, as the lift doors opened to reveal two porters with the young motorcyclist. One of them carried the young man's belongings and just for one moment, as she caught sight of the black crash helmet and leather jacket, Nadine's heart leapt against her ribs.

She turned away, sick at heart, and as she did so she caught Ruth's eye. For the first and only time since she'd known her Nadine caught a glimpse of sympathy on the other woman's face. Then the moment was gone and they pitched into the fray again.

The young man was admitted and prepared for Theatre and it was as Nadine finished taking his details and stepped out between the curtains, which she had drawn around his bed, that she became aware of a change of atmosphere.

Jayne and Lee were on the opposite side of the ward, tending one of the elderly passengers from the minibus, but they had both stopped and were staring towards the entrance. Ruth had just come out of the sluice and she, too, was staring open-mouthed down the length of the ward.

From where Nadine was standing she couldn't see the door and just as she was wondering what on earth could have happened to affect her staff in such a way she realised that they had turned and were all now looking in her direction.

Totally mystified, she stepped out from the curtained cubicle and looked down the ward.

Because she had been thinking about him, just for a second it seemed the most natural thing in the world that Angelo should be walking down the ward towards her. He looked exactly the same and, because she had seen him in this environment so many times before, he didn't look in the slightest bit out of place. The only difference now was that he wasn't wearing the white coat he had always worn before on Ortho. Now he was wearing a polo-necked shirt, expensively cut trousers and a tan-coloured jacket in soft leather.

Nadine's heart began to beat very fast as he drew closer.

He didn't take his eyes from her face, looking neither right nor left and seemingly oblivious to staff and patients alike.

And when he finally reached her and stood before her he smiled, the same old heart-stopping smile that had captivated her before—the smile she had come to know so well and which she had thought never to see again.

He stretched out his hand while she continued to gaze at him in a kind of numb wonder, unable to comprehend how or why he was there.

As if it had a will of its own she somehow found her hand in his, then he was drawing her down the ward towards her office—past the rows of beds and the patients, most of whom had no idea what was going on, and past the amazed but enthralled stares of the staff.

They reached the office, Angelo drew her inside, shut the door and then almost roughly pulled her into his arms, hungrily scanning her features.

'Angelo,' she whispered helplessly, 'what are you doing here?'

'What do you think I'm doing here?' he demanded.

'I don't know. . .'

'I get this crazy, crazy letter. . .I came to hear you say it was not true. . .'

'But, Angelo,' she protested, and was abruptly silenced as his mouth covered hers.

'Angelo,' she said again some moments later, 'the staff. . .'

'Damn the staff,' he said almost angrily, kissing her again. 'They can wait,' he added when at last he pulled away. 'This is far more important. I have to know, Nadine. I need to know. . .' A frown creased his forehead and the dark eyes were full of pain. 'You did not mean it. . . You did not mean those things you say. . .that you will not marry me. . .?'

'But. . .I tried to explain. . .'

'I thought you loved me.'

'I did. . .I do. . . Oh, you know I do, Angelo,' she cried. 'Please, don't make this any more difficult than it already is.'

'If you love me then nothing else matters.' He was gripping her arms so tightly that she winced with the pain.

'But there are so many problems,' she said hopelessly.

'No problem is too big if we love each other,' he insisted.

'But your family, Angelo. It is obviously important to them who you marry; that you marry someone who will give you children. . .a son to carry on the Fabrielli name. I doubt I can do that.'

'You tell me this before. . .I tell you then it does not matter. I tell you the same thing again. It is you I love, Nadine; you I want to marry. It is nothing to do with my family.'

'But your sister, Maria, said it was all down to you to continue the Fabrielli bloodline. . . That your brother can't. . .'

'Listen,' he cut her short, putting his fingers across her lips, 'I am already in trouble with my father because I rebelled by becoming a surgeon and not going into the family business. What is one more rebellion?'

'But your mother. . .?'

'What about my mother?' His eyes narrowed.

'When she saw me. . .she seemed. . .'

'Yes?'

'I don't know,' Nadine shrugged helplessly again. 'She seemed disappointed. . .as if she had expected you to bring home a young girl. . .I don't think she even liked me, Angelo. I saw it in her eyes.'

'Now that is where you are wrong,' he said. 'Quite wrong. Absolutely wrong.'

'What do you mean?' She had turned away but she looked back at him now, mystified by the emphasis in his voice.

'My mother did like you. What you saw in her eyes was indeed disappointment but not for the reason you think.'

'I don't understand.'

'She was disappointed because she could not talk to you—get to know you. She was envious of Maria; that Maria could speak English and speak to you—something that she would liked to have done for herself.'

Far from convinced, Nadine fell silent.

'When I received your letter,' Angelo went on quietly, 'I was devastated. I get a visit at my apartment from my mother, and when I told her what you had said she said I had to come straight back here to see you.'

'She said that?' Nadine stared at him in amazement.

He nodded. 'She told me she had never seen me so happy as that day when she saw us together.'

'So, what did you say?' she asked weakly. She was beginning to wonder if all this was happening in a dream, and whether at any moment she would wake up and find that Angelo was far away in Italy.

'I told her I had already booked my flight to London,' he said. 'I told her I was coming back here to put everything right between us again.'

She stared at him, loving him—every part of him, from his dark eyes to his smooth golden brown skin and the thick black hair that curled against his collar. 'But what about our jobs?' she asked. 'What about Paul?'

'Before I came in here I went to see Seymour,' he

said. 'I told him everything, and he has offered me a place on his team here at Spencer Rathbone for two years. By then Paul will be at university, and who knows. . .? Maybe then you will be ready to come to Rome with me.'

'Angelo, you would do that for me?' Suddenly her voice was husky.

'Of course. I told you, I love you and I want to marry you.'

'Angelo,' she whispered, lifting her face for his kiss, 'I love you and I want to marry you too.'

'Well, I'm glad that is settled at last,' he said with a sigh. 'I was beginning to think you didn't like Italy, my apartment, my family or the Villa Fabrielli—but more than that I was beginning to think perhaps you didn't like me.'

'Oh, Angelo,' she whispered again in the second before his lips met hers, 'if you only knew.'

At last, reluctantly, they drew apart, Angelo opened the office door and they stepped out onto the hushed, silent ward.

Their happiness, however, was only too obvious for all to see and as they stood there, a handclap, at first solitary—started by Josh Barnes—was gradually taken up by the other patients and then the staff until, in the end, the entire ward rang with spontaneous applause.

Angelo, turning to Nadine, kissed her again—to the delight of all present. 'Just in case you were still in any doubt, Sister Hadley,' he murmured.

'How could I be, Dr Fabrielli?' she whispered. 'How could I be, after that?'

MILLS & BOON®

Medical Romance™

COMING NEXT MONTH

MISLEADING SYMPTOMS by Lilian Darcy
Camberton Hospital

How could Dr Megan Stone work with Dr Callum Priestley again, when she couldn't forget the night they had shared two years previously? Callum behaved as if nothing had happened, but now Megan really wanted him to see her as more than a colleague...

OUTLOOK—PROMISING! by Abigail Gordon
Springfield Community Hospital

Dr Rachel Maddox needed a quiet life after her divorce, and her new job and home seemed ideal—until Nicholas Page, eminent neuro-surgeon, began involving her in his life, and trying to organise hers!

HEART SURGEON by Josie Metcalfe
St Augustine's Hospital

Sister Helen Morrisey's sole aim was to be part of surgeon Noah Kincaid's team, because only then did she have a chance of regaining her small son from the Middle East. But she'd forgotten something important, and Noah offered to smooth her path—but what did he gain?

SISTER SUNSHINE by Elisabeth Scott
Kids & Kisses

Widower Dr Adam Brent was sure Sister Julie Maynard wouldn't cope with the job, but she proved him wrong, charming the patients, his two small children—and Adam! But he still wasn't prepared for commitment...

KEEPING COUNT

How would you like to win a year's supply of Mills & Boon® books? Well you can and they're FREE! Simply complete the competition below and send it to us by 31st October 1997. The first five correct entries picked after the closing date will each win a year's subscription to the Mills & Boon series of their choice. What could be easier?

$$6 + 3 + \square = 14$$

$$\square + 2 + \square = 15$$

$$\square + 1 + \square = 16$$

$$\square + 6 + \square = 17$$

$$\square + 3 + \square = 18$$

$$\square + 1 + \square = 19$$

$$\square + 5 + \square = 20$$

C7D

PLEASE TURN OVER FOR DETAILS OF HOW TO ENTER ☞

How to enter...

There are six sets of numbers overleaf. When the first empty box has the correct number filled into it, then that set of three numbers will add up to 14. All you have to do, is figure out what the missing number of each of the other five sets are so that the answer to each will be as shown. The first number of each set of three will be the last number of the set before. Good Luck!

When you have filled in all the missing numbers don't forget to fill in your name and address in the space provided and tick the Mills & Boon® series you would like to receive if you are a winner. Then simply pop this page into an envelope (you don't even need a stamp) and post it today. Hurry, competition ends 31st October 1997.

Mills & Boon 'Keeping Count' Competition
FREEPOST, Croydon, Surrey, CR9 3WZ

Eire readers send competition to PO Box 4546, Dublin 24

Please tick the series you would like to receive if you are a winner
Presents™ ❑   Enchanted™ ❑   Temptation® ❑
Medical Romance™ ❑   Historical Romance™ ❑

Are you a Reader Service Subscriber?   Yes ❑   No ❑

Ms/Mrs/Miss/Mr _____
                                                    (BLOCK CAPS PLEASE)

Address _____

_____

_____ Postcode _____

(I am over 18 years of age)

C7D